Through Five Yea   vel. She started writing during lockdown and has barely paused for breath since. When Kate isn't writing, she is herding eight cats – two of her own Dolly and Lola and six kittens that Lola produced after spending Valentines Weekend out on the tiles. Counting words has been replaced with counting kittens for the time being. She lives in Reading Berkshire, her adopted hometown and is immensely proud to call it her home. In her spare time, she reads avidly and plays computer games.

Glen: Because you really are a legend.

My three children – you are my love and my light.

Karen P: You saved my life – thank you forever.

Bob: Thank you for the singing in the dark – I love you.

Kate Barnham

THROUGH FIVE YEAR OLD EYES

AUSTIN MACAULEY PUBLISHERS™

LONDON • CAMBRIDGE • NEW YORK • SHARJAH

A CIP catalogue record for this title is available from the British Library.

ISBN 9781398456440 (Paperback)
ISBN 9781398456457 (ePub e-book)

www.austinmacauley.com

First Published 2023
Austin Macauley Publishers Ltd®
1 Canada Square
Canary Wharf
London
E14 5AA

I would like to thank the team at Austin Macauley for listening to the cries from the dark, and giving that small child her voice. Grace, for her support and positivity and throughout.

My two big sons – thank you for believing in me; you have made me so proud, and finally the best three grandsons any Nan could ask for keeping me sane and grounded whilst I wrote.

Part One

Maxine 1978

Twinkle twinkle little star.

The sea sparkles as if a million diamonds have been scattered across it, too beautiful to see without half closing my eyes.

I can feel the soft white sand between my bare toes and feel the warm salt laden sea breeze on my face.

There is a scent of candyfloss mixed with seaweed and diesel from the fairground over to my right.

I can hear the cries of the seagulls intermingled with the joyful screams of passengers on the fairground rides.

Someone is calling me, trying to snatch me away; I do not want to go.

"Get up!"

"Look at the state of this bed! Get up now!"

My mother's voice jolts me awake from my dream and immediately my senses are assaulted with sickening images of the night before. Being unable to move or breathe for the weight of my father's body taking up the space in my single bed. I cannot breathe, the weight of him is crushing me. My mind floods with the horror of what he did, what he made me do, what he said and how bad he smelt.

Twinkle twinkle little star…I hum under my breath with my eyes tightly shut desperately holding my breath, in the hope that I can replace the horrific images and odours with the dream I was so brutally torn from.

Gradually the images fade and I tentatively open my eyes and let go of my breath, allowing the morning to float in. The thin curtains are no match to the sunshine poking through and hurting my eyes, a whiff of an awful smell that I cannot comprehend.

My mind is closed but my body betrays me with the pain between my legs.

They feel as though they have been stretched wider open than was ever meant to be possible.

I can feel the soreness between them, on my face, chest and belly where he has rubbed his stinky self all over me yet again.

The corners of my mouth are split and caked with dry blood. My mouth is dry and coated with a vile salty taste that I can also feel sitting in my throat.

How did I get it so wrong again?

I washed and washed and washed myself.

I had no bad thoughts.

I blessed my mother and father in my prayers.

I made sure I did not walk on the pavement cracks.

I made sure I touched everything three times.

I made sure my dolls were lined up in the right order.

I made sure there was no room in my bed for him.

I prayed so hard and for so long.

I got it wrong again.

I grab Glonk my lucky pyjama case and hold him tightly to my narrow chest.

I am sorry, Glonky, I let you down.

Tears of self-pity well up in my eyes; I quickly sniff them back because I know how angry Mummy gets when I cry. Swiping the tears that have spilled out with the back of my hand, I get out of bed.

My pyjama bottoms are in a heap on my bedroom floor, I have no idea where my knickers are, I know I was wearing them last night I make sure of that, but they have gone.

My chest and belly feel sticky and I know that smelly stuff that came out of Daddy's thing last night will stay on me until I am next allowed a bath.

Twinkle twinkle little star.

Maxine 2018

I wake up with a start. My heart is thudding in my chest and I can feel the residue shame and sadness from my dream.

I switch my bedside lamp on and flop back onto my pillow in relief that I am a forty-five-year-old mother now, not that scrawny messed up five-year-old child anymore.

The dreams have been coming in more regularly since I took part in an initiative called The Silence Campaign. It was formed to research into the effects of childhood trauma on adults. I am not a survivor, we are all survivors, I just did my bit by talking to the counsellor about what happened to me at the hands of my father. What I thought, how I felt and what could have been said to me that would have made five-year-old me ask for help. Well, the short answer is nothing. It was not an entirely wasted opportunity though because I was able to tell them exactly that, there is no way a child will tell, it is up to the police, healthcare professionals and teachers to identify the signs. I did give them little signs to look out for, obsessive checking, counting, tapping, rocking and chanting, and simply take notice of the child that always seems tired, they've probably had their sleep disturbed.

Anyway, I am fine. I made the decision when I was sixteen years old that I would not think about it, nor would I let it affect me in any way; and it has not.

He stole my childhood; he was not allowed to take anything else from me.

After my interview with the Silence Campaign had ended, I felt euphoric because even though he had died from a massive brain haemorrhage twenty years ago and nothing would come of it, it was the first time ever that I had spoken to someone in authority about it and given his name, basically I reported him forty years too late.

My parents divorced when I was eighteen because he left my mother for another woman and being an only child, my mother leaned heavily upon me after that.

I told her about the sexual abuse he subjected me to because she was pining to have him back. I thought if I told her that, she would hate him as much as I do and be glad that he was now someone else's problem. She denied all knowledge of it. She even told me off for not speaking up sooner as she had a terrible life with him – her words, not mine and had I said anything she would have had a reason to get away from him. She showed no compassion for the child I had been, she focussed solely on her own self-pity.

I visit her every two weeks in the sheltered housing flat that I brought her five miles away from my home following her heart attack two years ago.

Moving her out of Reading and closer to me was not an entirely selfless act; it saved me the long uncomfortable drive back home with the constant reminder of all the awful memories of what happened there. I always returned with the feeling that I had been tainted somehow and that was the main reason for my escape to the Cornish coast when I was able to.

The sea had always been a source of comfort to me, so it was a dream come true to be able to uproot from Reading and live in a house where the beach is on my doorstep. Buying her the flat nearer to me was supposed to be enough but she does not stop complaining that she is nowhere near her friends and is lonely, something else for me to feel guilty about. She irritates me with her constant pity party about how dreadful her childhood had been at the hands of her mother and how she wished she had been blessed with more children. I find it difficult to hold my tongue with her and have lashed out more times than I can remember.

I always feel so guilty afterwards that I make myself spend more time with her and so the vicious circle carries on. Anna my daughter does not have any relationship with her because apart from when she was born my mother has never shown her any love or affection. As soon as Anna found her voice, she found fault with her and nit-picked. I did not see her for many years after she complained to me that Anna was precocious, and I was a rotten mother because I had allowed my child to have her own personality and opinion.

I left home and started my first job as a GPO telephonist the day after my sixteenth birthday.

I rented a bedsit near to the telephone exchange where I worked and although that was scary stepping out into the big wide world, it was not as scary as being at home with my parents.

I had hoped that my mother would at least miss me, but she did not.

I met Kevin at the disco in the local army barracks. When I saw this tall dark-haired, brown-eyed man wearing army uniform, looking at me, I was completely smitten at first sight. He was a man already at the age of eighteen.

I could not believe it when he came up to me at the end of the evening when the slow dance music came on and asked me to dance. My head did not even reach his shoulder. He walked me home that night and the kiss he gave me at my front gate terrified me with the onslaught of feelings so alien to me, that I pushed him away and ran into the house, slamming the door behind me.

He did not let that put him off. He pursued me relentlessly. Eventually I gave in and met him for a drink on a summer evening by the River Thames. He did not try to kiss me this time, but I was surprised by how disappointed I was by that.

Things progressed quickly after that evening to the point that I became not only comfortable with his physical displays of affection, but I wanted more.

I was very confused, on one hand I was terrified that going any further would repulse me, leaving me with feelings of guilt and shame because of what my father had done; but on the other hand, I needed to be physically closer to Kevin.

I did not see him for a few days but spent the time thinking about whether I really wanted to go the whole way with him. I did, but I was scared that it would remind me of the horrific abuse my father had subjected me to.

I forced myself to try to face the events that I had spent years trying to block; only to be flooded by guilt and shame. I became incredibly angry and frustrated with myself and raged that he was not going to impact on my adult life. I needed to be strong and not let him steal anything else from me.

Fate played her hand and the next time Kevin called me it was to tell me that he was being posted to Northern Ireland.

I was terribly upset because I knew he would be in danger and that once he had gone it would be at least three months before he would be able to return to Reading.

My mind was made up I was not letting anything come between us again.

It was not easy. I was so busy trying to block my father from my mind that I forgot to enjoy being that close to Kevin.

I enjoyed the cuddles afterwards more than the act itself; but I was proud of myself for being brave enough to go through it. I felt that Kevin had begun to erase everything my father did to me.

Kevin promised me that next time would be better.

It was.

We had three amazing weeks where we crammed everything we could into our relationship before he had to leave. I put all the horrible feelings about my father to the back of my mind and focussed solely on Kevin.

On our last night together before he left, he promised he would write every week and call when he could. I clung to him all night trying to brand into my memory the feel of his skin next to mine and the scent of Tabac aftershave and boot polish that was his unique smell.

When morning came, I would not look at him, I just told him to go and not to look back because I knew if I looked into those big brown eyes once more, I would be lost forever.

The three-month tour of Northern Ireland turned into six months, then nine months and before I knew it a year had passed.

I had done a lot of growing up in that time and realised that there was a lot of fun to be had out in the world, so I made the decision to cut ties with him.

By the time I was twenty-five, I knew I wanted to have a child of my own.

I had not been in any long-term relationships since Kevin and I decided to go our separate ways, but I knew enough about myself that I did not want a man in my life dictating how I should be or how I should live my life.

I had savings and had moved into a one bedroomed flat. When I realised, I was pregnant with Anna after a one-night stand on holiday my prayers were answered.

With hindsight, I can see how to people that did not know me or my history that would appear to be a selfish decision; I thought I was doing her the biggest favour ever, not having a father in her life.

I have been honest with her about the circumstances around her conception and apart from the usual problems when she hit puberty and decided that she was going to find her father and could not; we have managed alright between the two of us.

The situation has been easier on us because my darling nan left me her life savings and property in her will so money was the least of our problems.

The first thing I did was give notice on the flat I had been renting for the past seven years and left my job.

I decided to take holiday lets around the Cornish coastline until I found the house that I wanted to buy.

I was incredibly lucky that the second house I viewed was perfect. It needed a lot of work doing to it but that suited my purpose. I had always dreamed of my perfect home and knew exactly how it would look.

Downstairs is all open plan; with floor to ceiling glass sliding doors across the back looking out into the garden. The garden is all patio with old stock bricks making the garden walls. I have planters filled with sweet smelling herbs and flowers. Upstairs we have two exceptionally large bedrooms with en-suite bathrooms and in mine, my longed-for dream of a balcony that looks out over the beach and the sea.

For this, I will always be thankful to my nan.

There has been one other man in my life and despite us not being able to be together, he has remained the love of my life.

I first noticed Magos in a bar in the town centre five years before. It was getting to the end of the evening when I felt someone looking at me. I glanced across and this tall slim young man with long straight dark hair in a ponytail, was staring at me so intently that I had to look away. I was instantly overwhelmed with such a powerful urge to go over to him that it took my breath away.

"Oi! What is wrong with you? You look like you've seen a ghost!" commented my friend Karen who I'd come out for the evening with.

I was speechless and could only indicate with a swivel of my eyes in the direction of the bar where he was still standing.

"Oh my god look at him!" she exclaimed and promptly picked up her purse and went over to where he was standing.

I was consumed with embarrassment because she was bound to say something about my reaction to him, so I hurried off to the lady's toilet.

To my utter disappointment when I returned, he had gone.

The feeling of connection that I felt from him even though I had never spoken to him was so powerful it remained with me for days after.

I tried to put him out of my mind because he was clearly a lot younger than me and I was not looking for a relationship with anyone.

The following week, another friend along with a big bunch of people I did not know, invited me out to celebrate her birthday.

Anna was at a sleepover with her best friend, so I was grateful for the invitation of having some fun, rather than sitting in on my own.

When I caught up with them all at the bar we had arranged to meet at, it was clear that the celebrations had started much earlier in the afternoon. My friend and her group were so drunk that I decided to have the one drink to toast her birthday and make my excuses to leave.

I was waiting to be served with my drink when the bartender slid a glass of wine in front of me.

"Compliments of that gentleman."

He nodded to the other side of the bar. I looked over and with a thrill of excitement saw it was the young guy from my last night out.

The next thing I knew he was by my side.

He spoke in accented English and close I could see that he was much younger than me.

The evening passed in a whirl of shouted conversation and when he asked me to go home with him, I did not hesitate.

His bedsit was near the town centre in the less affluent part of town, but I did not care. I knew I was safe with him.

On that very first evening, I learned that he was thirteen years younger than me; twenty-seven to my forty. Even though we had connected so strongly, I did not for a minute think he would be interested in me because of the age gap. I was wrong.

We sat drinking mugs of tea in the glow of a Himalayan salt lamp and spoke about where our lives had led us up until that moment, until five in the morning.

As I got up to leave, he asked me what my name was; we had shared so much but not the most important information, it was as if we did not need to know the basic formalities; I told him and went to the door to leave, when he stopped me and asked for my phone number so that we could see each other again. I refused; it had been such a magical and spiritual evening I could not muddy it with that. I remember reasoning to myself that if I gave him my number and had to wait for his call or text and it did not arrive then the magic of that night would be lost.

He walked me to the taxi rank in the rain and just as the cab pulled up to take me home, he held me in his arms and kissed me in a way I had never been kissed before.

We had nothing in common, but I felt as though I had finally come home. Despite his age, he was very mature and very spiritual.

I learned that he was a practicing Reiki Master, and he was the only son of a British English teacher who met his Greek Cypriot dad whilst on holiday in Cyprus and had remained there ever since.

His father had died when he was young, but his mother had remained there where she had made her life.

Magos owned and worked from a Holistic shop in Cyprus but due to a recession there had come to England to work. He spent his time earning money working as a painter and decorator and flying home every six weeks or so to give support to his mum.

A month later I went out for the evening knowing I would end the night with him. I was right. This time I did not hesitate to give him my number.

The time we spent together was short; less than a year in all but it was truly the most beautiful time I have ever experienced.

I knew him, he knew me and there was no need for anymore words other than that.

The last time I saw him he said he had to go back to Cyprus for good. His mum was seriously ill, and he did not know if, or ever, he would return to England.

That night as I lay sobbing in his arms, he tenderly stroked my hair away from my face and told me that he had loved me before he met me and would forever love me. That we were twin flames and would have been together somehow in our previous lifetimes and we would be together again in our future lifetimes.

We parted the next morning without any promises to keep in touch because he was sure he would never return.

Three months later, I slam the front door as I come in, furious because someone has parked across my drive, forcing me to park on the road which means I will have to move my car when they decide to return. I have parked my car over theirs so they need to knock on my door should they want to leave at any time. Well, they will leave when I am ready. God help them, after I have taken chunks out of them, they will not do that again in a hurry.

I manage a shop for a local charity that supports a women and children's refuge. I have a team of brilliant volunteers and Olly is my only paid member of staff. He had previously enjoyed a great relationship with the ex-manager because they were both likeminded lazy people. They had run the shop to suit themselves, not bothered about the income needed for the suffering families; consequently, he was difficult to manage and had picked up some bad habits that I was struggling to get him out of.

He has been difficult to get on side resisting every single suggestion I have and causing unrest amongst the volunteers with his snipes and complaints about me. I feel I must tread very carefully around him as he will jump on the slightest thing that I say that he can twist to infer something else. It is tiring to say the least; I am always having to be on my guard and his constant lateness and being off on regular sick days makes him extremely unreliable.

Today had been particularly busy because Olly had yet again called in sick.

My patience has begun to wear very thin with him. When he does bother to turn up, he spends more time gossiping than he does doing any actual work. I am beginning to really dislike him.

A knock on the door made me jump out of my skin. I thrust it open to see an elderly couple on the doorstep.

"What?" I barked.

"Do you know who owns the yellow car that is blocking our car in?" a smartly dressed elderly man wearing a hat asked in a sheepish manner.

"Yes, it is mine." I state challengingly.

"Would you mind moving it please? We have been visiting our daughter and didn't know where to park, she's just moved in you see," he explains.

I tut as I grab my keys.

"Are you blind? Should you be driving if you cannot even see you are blocking my driveway?" I ask him angrily.

"No need to be rude!" his wife quavers, I turn my head and give her a cold stare.

"Shh, Marjory, get in the car," he whispers guiding her around to the passenger side of their car.

I jump into mine and reverse angrily, screeching my tyres and thrusting on the handbrake noisily while I wait for the doddery old fool to get in his silly car, with his silly wife, wearing his silly hat and get out of my way. He finally finds reverse gear and tiptoes his car out of the way.

I slam the car door with an unsatisfying thud and stamp back up to my front door, that gives a satisfying slam which partially alleviates my anger.

Only after I have slammed every kitchen cupboard door whilst making my cup of tea do I feel any better.

I go into my garden and light up a cigarette with a sigh of relief.

Maxine 1978

I put my pyjamas on to cover my nakedness and try to comb through my tangled blonde hair in an attempt to put right the ravages of the night before; not understanding that should anyone care to look into my eyes that the shame and guilt I carry is evidence for everyone to see.

No one sees me. I will not let them.

"Maxine! Wait there a minute."

I flinch as my teacher Miss Stacy touches my shoulder as I go to file out of class.

She is wearing a necklace that looks like rows of teeth and a jumper covered in a yellow daisy design; I must focus on that.

"Maxine?"

"Yes, Miss?"

I sit back down at my desk.

"Please come over to the reading room it's more comfortable on the cushions."

My heart is in my mouth and my tummy starts churning.

I do not think I can remember how to walk.

How to talk.

How to be.

"Come."

Miss Stacy holds out her hand to me.

I shake my head no.

I need Glonk. Where is Glonk?

Do not touch me.

Do not ask me.

Do not see me.

I follow her over to the reading room and sit by the window. I count the number of windowpanes and choose the third one to look through. I am tapping my leg one two three, one two three, one two three.

I hold Glonk to my cheek and repeat; twinkle twinkle twinkle, my mind refuses to grasp the rest of the nursery rhyme where it is in a stark panic.

I know I must have done something bad but as usual I do not know what I did.

Mummy says I do not know because I am stupid and too busy making up lies to listen.

I do not know why she tells everyone including me that I tell lies because I do not think I do.

Daddy says I must not tell anyone our special secret for if I do, I will be in big trouble.

He says the police will get me and put me in prison for telling lies.

Once, before I knew about the police and prison, I told Mummy my bed was messy and dirty because Daddy had been in it and I did not like it.

She locked me in my room for a whole day and night for telling lies.

I do not tell lies.

Twinkle twinkle little star.

Maxine 2018

I wake with a start. My body is soaked with sweat and I cannot move. It is pitch dark outside; I have no idea what the time is. I try to grasp the residue of the nightmare that I was having so I can try to make sense of it, to no avail. After a few minutes, the thudding of my heart slows down, and I can feel my arms and legs gradually relax. I stare into the darkness feeling more alone than I ever have, even though my twenty-year-old daughter Anna is asleep in the next room.

I leave my bedroom door open so our cat Belle can get in and out at her leisure and our golden Labrador Vincent can do his security checks as and when he needs to. They both sleep on my bed.

I notice movement in the dark hallway. I strain to see into the darkness but cannot make anything out.

I cannot just lay here whilst someone uninvited stalks through my house. Anger propels me out of my bed and I snap on the light. There is enough light to illuminate the hallway and I can see there is no one there. I put my dressing gown on and hurry out of my bedroom putting the lights on as I go. I do not feel scared I feel furiously angry.

"Get out of my house!" I shout in as menacing a tone as I can. I make my way angrily downstairs. I check the front door first which is still locked with both keys safely out of reach on the stairs. The back door is also still locked with dead bolts thrown across.

Nothing, no evidence of any intruders, and I cannot even blame Belle because she is still curled up in a basket of clean washing. I make a cup of tea and sit at the kitchen table feeling annoyed and frustrated that yet again I have had a disturbed night, it is becoming a regular occurrence.

I am only glad Anna has not been disturbed. I am having enough difficulty trying to work out what is happening to me without having to placate her too.

I spend the rest of the night huddled up on the window seat that looks out onto the sea, with Vincent curled up beside me.

As the sun starts rising wakening the birds, I go back to bed for the last couple of hours before I really must get up and face the day. As I make my way back into my room a stench so vile it immediately stops me in my tracks fills my nostrils. I check everywhere and cannot see where this awful smell is coming from. It seems to be surrounding me, in my hair, on my skin and I can taste it in my mouth. It is vaguely familiar and sparks a memory that I bat away; I am not going there after the night I have had. I climb back into bed bringing the duvet over my head to block everything out, and fall into a deep sleep.

Next morning, I am jerked awake by Anna calling me,

"Mum, it is nearly 8 o'clock!" and banging on my bedroom door.

"Oh, bloody hell I hate getting up late!" I moan as I crawl out of bed. I am not going to have time for a shower or anything I complain to myself.

I make a coffee and smoke a cigarette in the garden whilst I gradually wake up properly.

Anna knows to avoid me in the mornings, I do not like to speak until I am properly awake. Fragments of what happened in the night start poking at my consciousness. I am too tired to fight the images hijacking my mind. I feel waves of panic grip my whole body, I cannot breathe or move as terrible images torment my brain bringing with them the vile stench from the night before. Without realising, I drop to my knees on to the damp stone wrapping my arms around my body and rock back and forth humming tunelessly.

"Mum! What are you doing?" Anna's voice jolts me back into the morning.

Feeling the hard stone of the patio on my knees and the dampness seeping through my dressing gown I become aware of my surroundings.

"What the hell! Get up!" She continues, "You look terrible, do you feel ill?"

Embarrassed I sit back down on the garden chair and fumble for my now cold coffee.

"I'm OK, I just had a rubbish sleep last night," I mutter.

"Anyway, I am going to be late if I don't get a move on," I say in a falsely bright voice and make my way back into the house.

I usually walk to work purely so I can enjoy the walk home where I can disassemble the events of the day and enjoy my evenings without thoughts of work ruining my peace of mind. But today I must drive in because I do not want to be any later than I already am.

Olly turns up for his shift dead on nine thirty, I call him straight into my office to go through the reasons for his latest episode of sickness. It is difficult trying to get a straight answer from him because he goes around the houses describing everything but the reason why he was unable to work last week. I need to rein him in or we are going to be here all morning.

"Olly, just answer the question. Did you go to see your GP?"

"I was really ill and couldn't get off the toilet, I think I had food poisoning."

He offers with a grin on his face.

I let out a sigh of frustration.

"Answer the question!" I say sharply, he stares back at me and tilts his hat to the back of his head. I have told him not to wear it at work as it looks unprofessional but, that is another battle for another day.

"You think I'm lying; I have heard you have been moaning about me to the customers!"

He spits.

"I know people around here, they talk."

"I said did you go to see your GP?" I reply ignoring his accusation and looking back at the online sickness record I am supposed to be filling out with him.

Suddenly, I am assaulted with the vile smell from last night and again this morning. I look up puzzled as to where it has come from. He is tilting his chair onto the back legs rocking back and forth and looking at his phone; the smell is coming from him.

"Put that fucking phone down and sit on that chair properly!"

He looks up in surprise and puts the chair back on all four legs with a thud.

My heart feels as if it is trying to escape out of my body where it is beating so fast.

I cover my face with my hands when the realisation that I have lost my temper and sworn at him hits me.

"Oh God, Olly, I am so sorry; I shouldn't have done that," I whisper.

He gets up and slams out of the office. I look after him stunned with disbelief; did that just happen? Did I really let myself down so badly? I cannot believe that I have been stupid enough to play into his hands like that. Shame engulfs me and I drop my head into my hands and tear at my hair. I am fighting to stop the waves of panic engulfing me. I have embarrassed myself enough in the last twenty minutes, I need to take control. I sit for a moment taking deep breaths waiting until I can feel my heartbeat steady, and my hand that is tap tap tapping on the desk as though it has a life of its own, to still.

I investigate the mirror and see defeat staring back at me. Stupid, imposter, smelly idiot, useless, rubbish, pathetic, the thoughts crowd my mind on a wave of self-disgust and shame. I shake my head to disburse it and count, one, two, three, one, two, three, one, two, three repeatedly until nothing else can take up residence in my mind.

I open the door, go in search of Olly and find him in the yard on his phone.

"Olly in the office now!" I command.

He jerks his head up and looks at me with a sly grin, the stench is coming from him in waves and only serves to make my heartbeat faster with disgust.

He brushes passed me as he enters the office and it takes everything I have in me not to let him see how repulsed I am. He stands over me until I tell him to sit down.

Taking a deep breath, I begin.

"I am sorry I lost my temper."

"You swore at me!" he interrupts tipping his chair back onto the back legs.

"Yes, and I shouldn't have," I state, biting back the instant uncontrollable anger that has reared up in my chest.

"You have pushed and pushed your luck…" I begin but stop myself just in time before I play right back into his hands and do or say something else that could result in me losing my job. The thought of how much that would please him is enough for me to stop. For now, wiping that smug look from his face will have to be enough.

Taking a few shallow breaths so I do not inhale too much of the stench emanating from him in waves; I tell him he will not be paid for his last sick days and dismiss him from my office.

I can feel tears building up behind my eyes, but I bite them back. I will not give him the satisfaction of knowing he has got to me. Ever since I took this shop over, he has made my life as difficult as he can.

I go to pick up the phone to call Harry my boss, but it rings before I can pick it up.

"Good morning, you are through to Maxine at Children First, how can I help you?" I ask politely.

"Is that Children First?" a female voice asks.

"Yes, you're through to Maxine, how can I help you?" I reply.

She launches into a long monologue about what she wanted to donate and what we would give her in return for her donations.

This is an ongoing battle we have; people do not seem to grasp the concept of The Charity being for the children and families who needs our support but rather an opportunity for them to get cheap stuff or money back if they donate.

I finally get her off the phone, call Harry and fill him in about Olly's behaviour today and me losing it and swearing at him. He tells me what I already know about walking away or halting a meeting before tempers flared.

"It's just work, Max, you don't normally let this stuff get to you."

"I know but he is getting worse and worse, it is actually easier when he isn't in," I reply.

"I can't deal with him; can you have a word with him please?"

"You don't need me to sort it out, come on, Max, you eat people like that for breakfast!" he exclaims.

I know what he is saying is right, but my confidence has deserted me recently.

"Do you need to take some time off? When did you last take annual leave?"

I think for a moment before answering.

"No, I'm good, don't worry it's fine I've got this."

"Okay, take it easy," he replies and ends the call.

The phone rings as soon as I put it down.

"Good morning, Children First."

"Is that Children First?"

I sigh and reply yes, shaking my head silently at the ignorance of people.

I put the phone down and sit with my head in my hands trying to buck up the courage to go out to the staff area and make myself a coffee.

Minutes later with my shoulders back and my head in the air with a bravado I do not feel I have left the office. I leave the door ajar to get rid of the stench that Olly brought in with him, that is still lingering.

The day ends without further drama and I thankfully get into my car and pull out into the evening traffic when it is my turn.

From out of nowhere a white transit van comes at me at speed from my right, I scream and shut my eyes bracing myself for the impact. There is none. Slowly I open my eyes and the van is nowhere to be seen. The traffic lights are still red, nothing has moved. Nothing has changed.

That night I take three codeine tablets that I had left over following a bad tooth a year ago.

I had not liked taking them because they made me drowsy but that was exactly what I needed tonight. I was getting anxious about what the night was going to bring and knew enough that I was asking for trouble thinking that way.

I wake up the next morning to my alarm going off at seven. I am immediately relieved that I had not woken up in the night. That was all I needed a decent night's sleep to get me back on track. Anna is in the kitchen making coffee when I go down.

"Good sleep?" she asks as I sit down at the kitchen table.

"Yeah, not bad at all," I answer.

"You didn't hear the foxes last night then?"

I shake my head, no.

"They were really loud I am surprised they didn't wake you up."

"I'm glad they didn't, first decent night I've had in ages."

She laughs.

"Yes, I heard you snoring. Anyway, I'm off, see you later."

She grabs her bag and leaves.

I get on with preparing the beef for a stew that I am going to put in the slow cooker for dinner tonight.

It is lovely to come in and smell dinner already cooked for me after a long day.

Work is uneventful which is just as well as I feel a bit foggy from the overdose of codeine last night. Still, it is worth it I think, after I have had to re-read the same email for the fourth time.

It has been pouring with rain all day and I get drenched on my walk home from work. The smell of the beef stew that has been cooking all day greets me in a welcome wave of warmth and flavours. My parka and shoes are soaked through and the rain has even gone through to my dress. I switch the television and lamps on in the front room.

Grateful that the heating has come on already I go to my en-suite and run a deep hot bath. I pour in a generous measure of the expensive lavender oil Anna brought me last Christmas and get in for a long soak. The hot scented water relaxes my muscles and I feel a wave of contentment wash over me. The bath is positioned in the middle of the room and on a raised dais so I can enjoy the sea view whilst I relax.

I can hear my mobile phone signalling a text message downstairs; whoever it is can wait. I wrap up in my comfiest nightie and dressing gown and go downstairs in search of my slippers. I spot them by the front door where I took them off this morning and gratefully slip into them. The 6 o'clock news and weather report are warning of Storm Callum who is about to sweep across the Cornish coast where I live. I love a storm, the feeling that no matter who you are, what you have and where you are from, you will not be able to stop it. Nature at its finest putting us all in our places equally. Mother Nature, the great leveller.

I check my phone and see a text message from Anna, letting me know that she is staying at her boyfriend's place tonight because she does not want to get caught in the storm; and he lives nearby to where she works.

I dish myself a bowl of the warming beef stew, cut some of the bread I made the evening before and sit at the kitchen table to eat it whilst reading the book I have on the go. There is a loud clatter from the back door. Startled, I look up to see Belle has come through her cat flap with something in her mouth. She drops it on to the floor and looks up at me miaowing.

On the floor is the fattest longest worm I have ever seen. I really have not been able to stand them since a boy at school shoved a handful down my back in primary school. We had been making a wormery in class and it had been great fun to go and dig for worms in the school garden, collecting them up in a bucket ready for their new home, until he did that.

I quickly put a bowl over the worm so I could not see it, and to prevent Belle from playing with it, and went back to my unfinished dinner. I took a mouthful of the rapidly cooling stew and a vision of the worm under the bowl assaulted my senses. The chunk of beef from the stew in my mouth became the worm, I spit it out onto my hand with a cry of disgust and run to the kitchen sink to spit out the saliva that flooded my mouth. I rinse my mouth with a cup of cold water repeatedly to rid it of the taste and texture of the worm. My appetite gone; I scrape the rest of the stew into a food recycling bag and put it into the outside bin, because I cannot even bear to see it in Vincent's dish. I scrub the stew pot and my dish and spoon until not a trace of it was left.

Feeling a bit calmer I make a cup of tea and go through to the living room. Belle is in her usual spot right next to the coal effect gas fire that is blazing warmly. She pads up to me, butting her head on my face and purring loudly but, I push her away convinced I can smell the worm on her breath. I try to focus on the television, but images of the worm keep filtering across the screen. There is no way that I can uncover it let alone pick it up and put it outside, it will just have to remain there until Anna gets back tomorrow evening.

A loud tapping from the kitchen startles all of us. Belle runs upstairs leaving Vincent and I alone to deal with whatever or whoever is in the kitchen. My heart is in my mouth, but I must find out what is going on if I am going to be able to sleep tonight. Armed with just my phone I creep quietly into the kitchen. All is how I left it; the bowl is still there covering the worm. The under-cupboard lighting that I usually find soothing, casts shadows around the room turning everyday objects like the kettle, and the row of herbs I am growing on the windowsill, into something sinister. I turn the main light on and go to the back door. I cannot see any shape through the frosted glass, so I call out.

"Who's there?"

My voice sounds weak and reedy even to me, I am no match to anyone who wants to break into my house tonight. That thought brings with it a wave of sudden and intense anger. I am not cowering in my own house because someone is trying to get in. Furiously I unlock and wrench open the back door, immediately the wind and rain from the storm almost knock me off my feet. I slam the door shut, throwing the dead bolts with my heart thudding in my chest. I lean against it waiting for my heart and rapid breathing to steady. Out of the corner of my eye I see something move across the floor, a black crawling mass, there is a buzzing sound coming from it and the now familiar vile smell that I cannot seem to escape is all around me. It is spreading its way rapidly across the floor to my bare feet. I let out a scream and run to the other side of the kitchen and crouch in the corner; my skin is crawling with what feels like a million ants all over my body.

I cover my eyes cowering and rocking and humming to block out the horror.

Gradually my breathing and the banging of my heart slows to a more normal rhythm; sucking hungrily on my asthma puffer I tentatively open my eyes realising that the smell has gone and but for the sounds of the storm outside everything is as it should be. I scan the floor and walls for the black mass but there is nothing. A loud tapping comes from the back door again and it is a relief to see that it is nothing more than Belle's cat flap clattering in the wind.

Maxine 1978

"Maxine!"

Miss Stacy's voice sounds like she is drowning.

"I look up and she's staring at me, her eyes are shining like stars.

"You fell asleep in class for a little while today, didn't you?"

I put my head down in shame.

I do not remember being asleep. I remember being warm after school dinner and feeling sleepy, but I do not remember being asleep.

I must have been asleep if Miss says so.

I tug on Glonky's googly eyes and nod my head.

"Maxine, it is OK, you are not in trouble I just think maybe that I can help you."

I feel my face going hot and red and my eyes start burning.

Do not.

"Please, Maxine, if there is anything troubling you it is OK to tell me."

I do not understand why she is looking at me like that, I do not like it.

Leave me alone.

"I can't help you if you won't tell me."

I do not deserve help. If you knew about me and how bad I am you would hate me too.

I want you to stop looking at me. You might see me.

A smell floats on the air that I cannot quite put my finger on, but I know it is not good.

I turn to look out of the window, holding my breath, away from those eyes that are seeing too much of me. Tap tap tap. It is too late; a sudden sob forms in my chest and escapes through my mouth. I am feeling sorry for myself; Mummy says I am always feeling sorry for myself.

Panic starts to build in a tsunami of words, bad words, they start to clamour in my throat, tripping themselves up in a hurry to be heard.

If I let them out, she will never speak to me or look at me so nicely ever again.

She will say I tell lies and the police will put me in bad kid's prison.

Tap, tap, tap, one, two, three, one, two, three, one, two, three, I am rocking back and forth squeezing Glonky and humming to drown out the words.

Twinkle twinkle little star. How I wonder what you are.

Twinkle twinkle little star, how I wonder what you are.

Twinkle twinkle little star, how I wonder what you are.

Maxine 2018

I wake up suddenly cold and disorientated. I do not know where I am. I look around and I can see my bed with the duvet pulled back looking slept in. I am looking at it through the double doors that lead out onto my bedroom balcony.

With a start, I realise I am sat on the ledge of the balcony with a drop of twelve foot beneath me. I have knocked over my planters of lavender and lemon balm and there is mud on my feet.

I have an overwhelming urge to fall. Everything is silent; the storm has wreaked its vengeance and moved on. I suddenly realise that the noises in my head which are constantly clamouring for my attention have quietened at last. There is only one thought; let go, just let go and it will be over. I look down to the patio outside the kitchen door and notice that the garden furniture has been blown all over the place. Nothing is how it should be. I shake my head and tell myself to wake up it is just a dream. The goosepimples on my skin tell me I am not dreaming. Reluctantly, I climb down and get back into bed.

I call Anna as I walk to work the following morning and warn her about the worm that has taken up residence on the kitchen floor. She promises to move it when she gets home later in the morning.

The day at work passes quickly and I am grateful when I look at the clock and see it is already nearly 5 o'clock. Olly has worked well and been quite good company for a change.

Maybe he just needed to see a bit of fire from me, I do not know; but I still do not trust him.

As I am locking up, I suddenly remember that I had the heater on in the office all day and could not remember switching it off. I tell Olly to go; I unlock the doors and go back in. The lights take ages to come on properly, so I put my phone torch on and make my way through the shop. It is eerily quiet after the busy day we have had so I do not hang around. I can tell as soon as I enter the office that the heater is off, so I push the office chair away from it and leave. I am just about to open the front door when I have a vision that I have switched the heater on and pushed the office chair against it. I stand with my keys in my hand for a moment arguing with myself, knowing all the while that I will be going back in to check again. I do not bother with the lights this time and just use my phone torch. I suddenly become aware of an uncomfortable feeling that I am being watched. I am nowhere near the bank of light switches, so I hurry to the office, fumbling with the keycode numbers and getting it wrong twice before I manage to put the right code in. I check again that the heater is off and the chair is nowhere near it. I stand for a moment staring at the off switch to embed it into my mind, all the while aware of the uncomfortable creeping feeling that someone is behind me watching me. I really do not want to walk back through that shop in the dark with my phone torch creating sinister shadows. I am so annoyed with myself for not putting the main lights on so I try to focus on that.

It is with relief that I turn the final lock on the front door and leave, twenty-five minutes later than I usually get away.

Harry phones, about an area meeting that we are going to have in the next couple of weeks, to talk about the presentation I will be giving on health and safety. I am proud of my knowledge and am so deeply immersed in our conversation that I do not check both ways and just step out into the road. A white transit van appears out of nowhere just missing me and speeding off down the road. I let out an involuntary scream and drop my phone, causing a crack across the screen. I scrabble to pick it up heart pounding at the near miss, I can hear Harry is still talking so not only did he not hear me embarrassing myself, but the phone still works. I end the call and looking both ways; one, two, and three times I cross the road.

I can smell that Anna has prepared dinner as soon as I walk through the front door.

"I've run you a bath, Mum!" she calls from the kitchen, Anna code for do not disturb me whilst I am cooking. I smile to myself because even though she does not cook as often as I would like her to, it is always worth the wait.

I come downstairs after my bath to a steaming plate of homemade chilli con carne. The kitchen looks like a bomb has gone off in it because she uses every saucepan, dish and utensil and does not load the dishwasher as she goes. I sit down and dig my spoon into the rice.

"Oh yeah! I got rid of the worm; it was tiny!" She laughs.

I nod my grateful thanks because my mouth is full. Immediately, the rice starts to writhe on my plate like a mass of maggots, crawling about all over each other in a stinking heaving mass. I gasp and run to the sink to spit out the mouthful of maggots that had disguised themselves as rice. I run the tap quickly and grab a glass and gulp down the water.

"What's wrong with it?" Anna asks with concern.

"Don't you like it?"

I do not know what to say, not only will I sound crazy if I tell her, but I will put her off her dinner too.

"It's fine, it's lovely, I just got some stuck in my throat."

I sit back down at the table and mix the rice with the sauce and try to finish eating it. Thankfully, Anna is oblivious and does not notice me pushing my dinner around my plate and not actually eating it. When she has finished hers, I tell her that I will sort the kitchen out seeing as she cooked and shooed her out of the way. I guiltily scrape my plate into the food recycling bag and put it outside in the bin. Noticing the garden furniture has been blown all over the garden, I remember the events of the night before. Was that a dream? Or did I really wake up in the middle of the night trying to throw myself off the balcony?

Maxine 1978

I can hear someone moving around my bedroom, but it is too dark to see. I can smell hair cream, sweat, cigarettes and farts, it is him. My heart is racing, and my body goes hot and cold in fear and panic. I squeeze my eyes tightly shut and gently let go of the breath I have been holding, maybe he will leave me alone tonight if I do not make a fuss and cry and beg him not to, just be asleep, not wake up and make a fuss.

He is not alone. He has got someone with him. I am scared, this has not happened before. Then I hear them talking quietly. My heart leaps in my chest, it's Mummy! She has come to stop him and save me! I let out an involuntary whimper and I sense them still, listening. The floorboards creak, someone is coming up to the bed. I scoot across to the wall and huddle clutching my knees to my chest with my head resting on my knees. They must be able to hear my heart banging so loud.

Suddenly, the blanket is ripped away from my body, causing a shock to reverberate through me.

"Caught you! I knew it! Playing with yourself, nasty dirty little girl"! says my mother with a triumphant tone to her voice with that she drags me by the shoulder away from the wall.

He is standing behind her with his big torch shining on me. As I open my eyes the beam is too bright and I shrink away from it and them. I grapple for my blanket but she snatches it away and moves to the door with it.

"Dirty little girls can't have blankets, can they, Daddy?"

Maxine 2018

I wake up with a jolt with my duvet grasped tightly in my hand. Sweat pours from my body soaking my night dress and the sheet beneath me. My mouth is open in a silent scream, my arms and legs rigid in terror. |The faint tinkle of a nursery rhyme whispers in my ear with sinister intent.

The feel of my full bladder propels me out of my bed; as I make my way to the bathroom, I become aware of something in the hallway sitting in the corner near the ceiling watching me. The vile smell that seems to follow me no matter how many times I shower and bath. It is emanating from there. The nursery rhyme Twinkle twinkle little star floats across my consciousness and I know that sound is coming from the thing up there in the corner. That thing which constantly follows and watches me and I know with complete and sudden clarity it wants to possess me.

I wake the next morning feeling as though I have been hit by a bus. I drag myself out of bed and into the shower to try to dispel the feeling of shame that seems to cling to me.

I leave my nightie and knickers on in the shower because that thing is everywhere and it cannot see me naked.

I am getting scared now.

The walk to work is eventful because the white transit van is coming at me out of everywhere. I am starting to think that maybe it does not exist outside of my mind, but the fear, feeling and sound of the impact is all too real.

Later, I am sitting in the work yard with a much-needed coffee and cigarette when I have the sensation of jolting back into my body. I immediately notice the feel of the wooden seat beneath me, the cigarette smouldering in my hand and the taste of coffee on my lips. I feel disorientated and shaky.

I am starting to think that I am losing my mind.

One of the volunteers comes out to let me know that a customer wants to speak to me.

I spray my body mist to mask the smell of cigarettes and go onto the shop floor. A middle-aged man wearing a pork pie hat is waiting by the sort room door. I go to pass him but he stops me by laying a hand on my arm. The smell is back and it is coming from him in sickening waves. I jerk back to remove his arm but he steps closer to me. His beady eyes glint behind his wire framed glasses and I can see the remnants of his last meal around his mouth. He mumbles something that I cannot quite catch so I ask him to say it again.

"I wondered if you could help me, you see, I'm a big rock music fan and I am looking for a book called *1978 what a year that was*, take my number and let me know if you come across it, I'll make it worth your while," he mutters.

"All our books are over there," I say pointing to the front of the shop whilst trying to move away from him.

"Listen…" he begins and once again touches my arm and invades my personal space, I jerk backwards away from him.

"Back off, stop touching me!" I shout loud enough for the whole shop to hear.

He reels back in surprise.

"I was only asking."

"No, you were getting nearer and nearer to me and I told you. Back the fuck off now!"

"You can't swear at me! I am a customer; the customer is always right!" he stutters.

I walk off, grab my cigarettes and phone on the way and kick the yard doors open.

Dai one of the workers from the supermarket next door is also out in the yard enjoying his break.

"You alright? You look like you want to kill someone!" He laughs awkwardly.

Angry tears well up in my eyes which I brush angrily away. I do not cry and I am fucked if I am going to let that paedo creep make me cry. I shake my head and light my cigarette, after a couple of puffs I feel the anger start to simmer down I look across at Dai.

"Just customers, you know. Always being right!" I say with a slight laugh.

Maxine 1978

I am in the classroom on the last day of term, everyone is happy and full of chatter about the long summer holidays ahead.

There will be no learning class today, it will be a day filled with fun and games and everyone is happy but I am not.

44

I know I am spoiling it for everyone because Miss just asked me why I am sad and everyone looked at me.

I do not like it when they look at me, they can see how nasty, dirty and smelly I am, so I go and hide in the cloakroom. I need to clean myself, so I do not infect everyone else with my shame and guilt. I take my shoes and socks off and start washing my toes, then legs, arms, tummy and face. I have a nasty taste in my mouth where Daddy put his thing in it last night. It has made the corners of my mouth crack, bleed and be sore.

I am nearly done when I hear someone push the door open.

"Maxine? What are you doing?"

Miss Stacy comes in and makes me jump.

I shake my head, no. My cheeks are bulging and my eyes are stinging.

She comes closer to me, so I back away until I am pressed up against the sinks and can go no further.

"Whatever you have in your mouth I need you to show me, Maxine."

I shake my head. No.

"Maxine?"

I can see what looks like disgust and hate that makes her eyes wet when I take the piece of soap out of my mouth.

Maxine 2018

I wake up and immediately feel relieved to realise that it is my day off. I stretch luxuriously and promise myself that once I have done all my chores in the correct order then I can have a nice relaxing day.

I put a piece of gammon in the slow cooker first thing so that it can do its business whilst I do the housework and washing. I love cleaning and keeping things in order. I cannot relax until everything is done.

I have just finished putting clean sheets on my bed when a fragment of last night's nightmare hijacks my mind. I frantically push it away; nothing is going to spoil my enjoyment of my mood today and it was only a nightmare. I force myself to think about what I need from the supermarket later.

Forty-five minutes later, I am just going out of the front door when I spot something moving on the stairs. I put my bag down and go up for a closer look. As I get nearer it fades from my vision, I blink a couple of times and start to feel ever ready anxiety claw at my stomach. I look again, there it is, a heaving crawling mass of blue bottles, I can smell them rotting. I run to the kitchen, grab the fly killer from under the sink and a tea towel to cover my mouth. Where did they come from? I have literally just finished cleaning and bleaching the entire house.

Realisation hits me like a punch in the face. There is nothing there.

A huge lump fills my throat and hot tears prick my eyes as I realise there is no way I can face the supermarket right now. My day has been ruined after all. This thing whatever it is, is taking over, stealing my sleep, my life and my mind.

The box of codeine is still reassuringly full. I pop two out and swallow them down with a cup of tea sweetened with honey and go into the garden chain smoking in the cool autumn air.

An hour later and the tablets still have not worked their magic, so I go to take two more. The thing that watches me in the corner at night now appears to be following me around no matter where I go; making its presence known by the stink it carries with it.

The slam of the front door shocks me out of my contemplation. With a jolt, I realise Anna is home from work already. How have I lost over four hours of my day? The last thing I can consciously remember is getting ready to go to the supermarket. The box of codeine sits accusingly on the garden table in front of me. I cannot remember if I took the extra dose or not. The sound of Anna coming out into the garden prompts me to guiltily hide them in my coat pocket.

"I am absolutely starving!" she states as she flops down into the chair opposite me.

"Anyway, what are you doing sitting out here? It's freezing."

I point towards the old jar that I throw my cigarette stubs into and shrugging my shoulders, I get up and go back in.

I am making an old family favourite for dinner tonight. Gammon ham, mashed potatoes and boiled eggs. Thankfully, I had managed to take the meat out of the slow cooker earlier without even realising that I had, so it was nicely rested rather than overcooked and ruined as I had dreaded.

"You OK?" Anna queries as she starts laying the table.

"You seem preoccupied?"

"I'm, umm, just busy, I'm fine don't worry, love," I say brightly sticking a fork into the meat to hold it steady whilst I carve thick slices.

As the sharp knife carves through the pale pink flesh of the gammon, unbidden thoughts fill my mind of my knife

47

slicing easily through human flesh. Horrified I drop it with a clatter on to the floor. The aroma of rotting human flesh fills my nostrils and turns my stomach inside out. I flee to the toilet heaving; hoping that Anna has not noticed, so I do not have to explain the madness and horror of what has just happened.

Thankfully, she is still engrossed in busily tapping away at her iPhone when I return and has not noticed anything.

I dish out the dinner a few minutes later and sit down to eat. I cover the meat with pickle to disguise the gleaming pink flesh. My stomach is still churning and a layer of sweat beads my face as I begin to eat. I put my knife and fork down and go to the sink for a glass of water and sitting back down, I quickly cut a chunk of gammon, ignoring the horrific taunts in my head and start to chew. The images come in thick and fast that I am eating my own flesh, so I grab the kitchen paper towels and spit the mouthful out into it. My heart is hammering away in my chest and any appetite I had has completely gone.

I switch the kettle on and start to load the dishwasher. Anna has completely cleared her plate and has gone upstairs to freshen up after her day at work.

I can usually make a piece of gammon last a couple of days and will take the last few slices to work in a sandwich but I know I will not be doing that now. I quickly bundle it into a food recycling bag and put it in the bin outside. I am dismayed to note that for the first time ever the bin is overflowing.

I sit down on the back doorstep and the tears that I have held back for so long course down my cheeks. I do not know what is happening to me, I am convinced that I am going mad. My mind fills with all the horror that it has visited upon me recently, the sights, sounds and the ever-present vile smell until it completely overwhelms me. I sob into my hands rocking back and forth until I have no more tears left to cry.

Anger starts to build in my belly; rising until it obliterates everything. I smash my mug of tea onto the path and kick over the food recycling bin. The garden furniture is next as I hurl it into the brick garden wall with a scream of rage.

As suddenly as it arrived the anger leaves, leaving me utterly exhausted.

I go upstairs and still in the clothes I have worn all day fall into my bed and a deep sleep.

Maxine 1978

As I leave school I search for Daddy's big white van. But I cannot see it anywhere.

I am happy he is not picking me up; I hate seeing him and his hat at school infecting everything and making it seem dirty.

I see Mummy is waiting for me by the school gates when the bell goes, so I must hurry.

I like it better when she picks me up.

I gather up my paintings and workbooks and rush out of the door.

I hope she likes looking at my work.

Miss Stacy tries to stop me, but I cannot stop I have to go, or Mummy will be cross.

Mummy is with Nicole's mum; they are so deeply engrossed in their conversation that they do not see either Nicole or I.

Miss Stacy suddenly appears in front of us.

"Can I have a word please, Mrs Adams?"

Mummy stops mid-sentence and glares at her.

"I will only keep you a moment. I…"

"What is it? Is she playing up as usual, is she? I was just saying to Babs here about the lies this one comes out with!"

"No not at all, look can we go back into the classroom and discuss this privately, Mrs Adams?"

I have never seen Miss Stacy look like this. Her face has gone red and her body looks all tense and angry.

Mummy nods her head sharply and we follow her back into the school.

Mummy makes me wait outside.

School feels different now, all echoey and quiet. I miss the noise, and the smells seems much stronger now.

I wish they would hurry up. I want the toilet badly. I am scared to go because if Mummy comes out and I am not here I am in big trouble.

I can hear Mummy talking in the posh voice she uses when she is speaking to the doctor, but I cannot make out what she is saying.

Suddenly the door opens and both Mummy and Miss Stacy appear. Both are smiling but not really. I can tell I am in big trouble. Miss Stacy bends down and takes my hand.

"I won't be seeing you after today, Maxine, Mummy has told me that you are moving to a new house during the holidays. I hope you have a lovely summer holiday and that you like the new school you will be going to in September."

I do not know what to say. I did not know we were moving to a new house.

I do not want to not see Miss Stacy again, I do not want a new school with new people, new children, new teachers. I am so confused. Mummy suddenly pulls me away and hurries out of the school holding my hand very tightly.

I look back to see Miss Stacy standing where we left her and she looks like she is crying.

I want to run back to her, to finally bury myself in the arms that I have longed for but been unable to do so for so long. To smell her perfume is the only thing that can block out the other horrible smells that follow me around.

A lump in my throat threatens to choke me but I know I must not cry. I am in enough trouble as it is.

I hate myself, why am I so stupid? Why can't I get anything right? Why am I so thick, slow and stupid? I hate my stupid voice all blocked up with snot all the time. I sound so stupid it makes Mummy angry.

Mummy is dragging me and walking so quickly that she is going to pull my arm off in a minute.

She is making me step on all the cracks. I begin counting. One, two, three, one, two, three, one, two, three, my face burns and my chest is tight where I am running out of breath trying to keep up with the tug of my arm.

I start coughing and wheezing. It is hard to get a breath in and I feel the trickle of urine down my leg.

I start crying and pleading but she just looks at me with disgust.

She is furious with me but I cannot help it. She unlocks the front door and pushes me inside.

"In. Go to your room, you dirty little girl. Your father will be dealing with you," she mutters through gritted teeth.

"Mummy, Mummy!" I sob through the wheezing of my chest.

The slap comes from out of nowhere and I hit the opposite wall. To my shame more urine cascades down my legs puddling in my school shoes and on the hallway carpet.

She is in the kitchen and I can hear her rummaging through the kitchen drawer.

She grabs me so I am held high and away from her whilst she beats me repeatedly with the wooden spoon.

"Attention seeking little bitch! Whining to your teacher about us? What did you think was going to happen? Hey? Did you think you would get away with it? That she wouldn't guess what a dirty nasty little girl you really are."

"Let me tell you, she knows exactly what you are now. She does not like you either. She said you are thick and stupid and ugly; she wishes that you were a nice girl like Nicole! She is glad she does not have to deal with your snivelling anymore! No one likes dirty little girls who tell lies. Do they? Do they? Answer me!"

"No, Mummy."

"What are you?"

"A dirty little girl, Mummy."

I sob.

Each word is accompanied by a slap with the wooden spoon and flecks of her spittle cover my face.

When she has exhausted herself, she throws the wooden spoon at me and through tight lips tells me to get out of her sight.

I crawl up the stairs to my room and remove my wet clothes. I put my pyjamas on and go into the bathroom because there is a lock and I can be safe for a bit. One, two, three, one, two, three, one, two, three, tap, tap, tap, I am going tap, tap, tap, go, go, go. I squeeze my eyes tight blocking out the squalor and filth of the bathroom and will myself away.

Twinkle twinkle twinkle.

I can feel something pushing at my back. I come to my senses and hear my father's voice coming from behind the bathroom door.

"She's blocked the door, Ruth. Little bitch has barricaded herself in there! Open this door NOW!" he commands.

I struggle up to pull the bolt back and he thrusts the door open nearly knocking me down. In my haste, I drop Glonk as I scrabble to get away from him.

He grabs the front of my pyjamas and hoists me out. He still has his hat on, he hardly ever takes it off. Mummy calls it a porkpie hat. It does not look like a porkpie to me.

I can tell by the look on his face that he is enjoying this and by the way he has tilted his hat to the back of his head.

"Dumb insolence!" he cries to my mother who is hovering around behind him.

They both seem strangely excited. I know what this means. I try to make myself small so that they cannot see me, but it is fruitless; they are always looking at me. Where is Glonk? I look around in panic. I need Glonk. Tap, tap, tap.

"Mummy!" I appeal to her because what will happen next will be so horrible, I will try anything to stop it.

Their little games that they enjoy so much are getting worse. They think things up that I cannot second guess, so I am never prepared.

"Mummeee please!"

"Don't you Mummy me!" she mocks in a nasty nasally voice.

"Mummeeee!" It is his turn now mimicking my blocked nose and pathetic pleading voice.

I don't know what to do, how to be, where to look, what to say – tap, tap, tap.

I don't want to be seen. Tap, tap, tap.

Involuntarily I tap my head, One, two, three, one, two, three, one, two, three rocking back and forth and humming to block out their laughter.

Twinkle twinkle little star, twinkle twinkle little star, twinkle twinkle little star, faster and faster, rocking harder and harder and harder.

"Enough! Come here!" he snarls in a low voice.

Mummy seems to sit up a little straighter. Her eyes are shining with happiness as she looks at him.

Why does she never look at me like that? Why doesn't she like me? Why can't I be like Nicole? Mummy likes Nicole she wishes I would be like Nicole.

He is taking the clock down from its nail on the wall, smirking and staring at me.

I stand before him not knowing what is coming next, trying to control the shivers that highjack my whole body.

I tighten up my arms my legs my back so I can be as still as a statue, but my jaw has a life of its own chattering my teeth so hard, I am scared that they are going to fall out.

I can smell him; sweat and cigarettes. Stale farts and staler breath.

He turns me around and bunches the back of my pyjama top into a knot. I cannot keep still, the trembling is out of my control now.

He looks across to her with raised eyebrows, she gives a nod.

He lifts me up by my knotted pyjama top and snags it onto the nail in the wall where the clock usually hangs.

My legs are kicking but there is nowhere for them to take purchase.

My face is red and hot, and I can feel my pyjama trousers slipping down. I stop.

I cannot raise my head…

The last thing I notice is them lighting up cigarettes and him settling his hat squarely on his head.

Twinkle twinkle little star.

Before I know it, we are on our way to our new house in Liverpool. Daddy has a job there at a children's home.

We arrive at a tiny little house that is squashed between two others and go in. Mummy said we are renting it and she is not overly impressed with its small pokey rooms.

After the summer holidays, I must go to my new school that is at the end of the road we are living on. Part of me is really scared but another part of me is incredibly happy. Daddy has not been into my room and tried to play his night-time games with me at all since we came to live here.

He goes to work at night-time and sleeps in the daytime.

Mummy says I must keep very quiet and must not wake him up.

I am good at being quiet.

I am also good at not stepping on the cracks in the pavements.

I am careful to touch things three times as well.

I learnt a rhyme that makes it easy.

Once a wish, twice a kiss, three times lucky.

It has finally worked.

Glonky has looked after me very well.

Maxine 2018

I wake up in the morning feeling more tired than I did when I went to bed last night. My swollen eyes and chapped red face in the bathroom mirror reflect the ravages of the night before, causing red hot anger to rise in my belly and fill my head.

Everything in me is telling me not to go to work in this state of mind but that only makes me angrier. I know I am in no fit state to drive so I literally storm up the road to work.

As soon as I get into the shop, I can see that closing down was not done last night. There are clothes on the floor and donation bags left by the till. The staff area is a mess of overflowing bins and unwashed coffee cups. In a fit of rage, I gather everything up and throw it in the bin outside.

I go into my office to write a fuming email ready to blast Olly out of the water when the phone rings.

"Good morning, Children First."

A dead silence and the phone being put down is the response. I do not care I am not in the mood to speak with anyone just yet, so I put the phone off the hook until I have had a coffee and cigarette.

My head is pounding and my stomach is churning as if I have a hangover.

I have no idea how I am going to get through the day and my anger will not let me keep still.

Olly comes in full of himself and immediately I recognise the vile smell that is coming from him in waves, it is an old familiar mixture of stale fags, farts and sweat. As he comes near to me it gets stronger. I put my hand over my nose and mouth and recoil in disgust.

"Where's my Superman mug?" he asks belligerently coming ever closer to me.

I glare at him back.

"In the bin with the rest of the fucking rubbish you left lying around last night!" I retort.

He looks around him as though searching for moral support. He opens his mouth to answer but I shut him down.

"I do not expect to come in after my day off to clean up after you, Olly!" I spit out.

"I had a dentist appointment, an emergency on…" He is interrupted by the phone ringing. I snatch it up.

"Good morning, Children First, how can I help you?" I snap.

I am greeted by a moments silence.

"Is that Children First?"

I look at the phone in disbelief and throw it as hard as I can against the office wall. Olly jumps back in surprise.

"Hey that nearly hit me!" he exclaims.

Suddenly the fog in my brain clears and I know without a shadow of doubt what I need to do.

Picking up my bag and parka I look him dead in the eye and say, "I don't fucking care!"

I leave the shop in a wave of euphoria without looking back.

I switch off my mobile phone and make my way home.

It feels strange to be walking back the way I have only just come, and I am not even surprised when the out-of-control white transit van mounts the pavement heading straight for me – let it do its worst. I brace myself for the impact.

Seconds later I become aware of high-pitched wailing. A woman walking her dog on the other side of the road crosses quickly and puts her hand on my arm and asks me if I am alright, it is then I become aware of the tears and snot cascading down my face and realise that the wailing is coming from me.

Later that day I switch my phone back on to text messages and a voicemail from Harry asking me to call him. I have nothing left in me to be nervous or worried about his reaction to my behaviour earlier today.

Obviously, Olly would have been straight on the phone to him no doubt exaggerating the already appalling incident.

"Hello!" I say tonelessly when he picks up on the first ring.

"Maxine, finally. I have been so worried. Are you alright?"

The kindness and concern in his voice brings on an onslaught of tears, I can hardly get my words out.

"Shhh, Shhh, its OK, breathe," he says gently triggering an instant panic attack so severe I think I am having a heart attack.

I drop the phone and try to catch my breath not even aware of the tiny sound of Harry's voice telling me to stay where I am, he is on his way.

The sudden rap on the back door makes me jump out of my skin. I am huddled in the corner of the kitchen, knees to my chest and my arms wrapped tightly around me. I have no recollection of how long I had been there or why. I stand up too quickly and immediately feel dizzy so I sit down at the kitchen table with my head in my hands.

The back door opens slightly and Harry peers around the door.

"Max, can I come in?"

I look over my shoulder at him dully, I am not even sure if this is real, or I am imagining it.

The smell of his after shave on the October air is a welcome reminder that the farts fags and sweat smell is not present right now.

He busies himself with the kettle chatting brightly as though it is completely normal for him to be making coffee in my kitchen when we are both supposed to be at work.

Finally, he places my cup in front of me and the smell of the fresh coffee reminds me that I need a cigarette. I pick my cup and cigarettes up and signal that I am going into the garden for a smoke. He follows me out and I can see the look of horror on his face when he takes in the food rubbish and garden furniture strewn everywhere.

He busies himself clearing up and righting the furniture whilst I watch him, smoking my cigarette from the back doorstep. When he is done, he sits on one of the garden chairs and just looks at me. I mutter thanks red faced and embarrassed that he has seen me and my garden in such an awful state.

"What happened, Max? And I don't mean about at the shop today, I mean what happened to you?"

I shake my head; I have not worked it out for myself yet let alone have the words to explain to anyone else. He looks at me kindly.

"I want you to self-certificate, Max, take some time to yourself without the bullshit and pressure of work."

"I can't…" I begin but he cuts across me.

"You can and you will. Do not worry about the shop, I will deal with that. I just think you need a rest; it's all come on top of you, hasn't it?"

I nod dumbly.

"And, Max, I really think you should make an appointment with your doctor, get yourself checked out, OK?"

"I don't need the doctor, there's nothing wrong with me, I probably just need a couple of days off together," I offered.

"OK, but listen, I don't want you back in that shop until next Monday, do you hear me?" he says kindly.

I mumble my thanks as a wave of relief floods over me. I feel like a heavy load has been taken from me.

"I am really sorry about this and everything, and losing it at work today," I say.

"Think nothing of it, Max, you are the best store manager I have and I know you wouldn't lose it without good reason. Anyway, I better go, Anna is still living at home, is she?"

I confirm with a nod.

"I will check in with you on Friday, but if you need anything, even just to talk, call me any time."

With that, he gets up and goes.

I sit on the doorstep for a bit longer trying to assimilate what has happened today. I left for work at 8 a.m. not even guessing that I would be back home with my tail between my legs four hours later.

The rest of the day passes in a daze. I cannot do anything but pace around the house with a bottle of bleach and a cloth cleaning away every speck of dust I can find.

Anna comes in and can tell straightaway I have been home all day.

"I thought you were at work today?" she says putting her bag down on the kitchen table that I have just bleached.

"Noooo!"

I rush to move it from my clean and tidy surface. She looks at me in disbelief and slowly takes her bag and puts it on the floor.

"Okay, you need to listen to me, Mum," she says pulling out a kitchen chair and forcing me to sit.

"You need to go to the doctor and get some help."

"Has Harry phoned you?" I interject.

"What? No! What's happened?"

I reply, "Nothing," turning away from her.

She shoots out of her chair and comes over to me and pulls my long blonde hair away from my neck.

"What's that on your neck?"

She leads me to the mirror by the back door and lifting my hair away from my neck I can see large scratches and gouge marks all around it.

I am horrified. I have no idea where they have come from and the ones under my ears look deep.

"Has someone hurt you?" she asks tears filling her eyes.

"Oh God, someone's attacked you and you haven't told me!" she wails.

"I've heard you screaming in the night loads of times!" she groans.

"Why didn't you tell me?" she ends on a sob.

"I promise you, Anna, no one has attacked me. I have been having some really bad nightmares and it's got on top of me a bit so it's probably from that."

I go to the sink to fill the kettle and with my back to her I carry on.

"I have lost it at Olly a couple of times lately and ended up walking out today."

"Harry's alright about it; he came around today and told me to self cert for the rest of the week."

I finish, setting down a mug of tea in front of her.

"That little shits had it coming; the crap he gets away with."

"Yeah, but I was really unprofessional."

"As long as Harry is on your side it doesn't matter," she replies, then with a little grin.

"Go on, what did you do?"

An hour later, I am feeling much better after describing to Anna my losing it at work.

She is laughing so much that she starts me off and the tension of the day seeps away.

I feel a bit better knowing that I do not need to go to work in the morning, so we order a takeaway and have a good evening watching Netflix.

Maxine 1978

I do not even get to go to my new school in Liverpool because after we have been there for about four weeks Daddy comes home from work early.

It is getting dark and I have been in bed for ages. It is difficult to get to sleep when it is the summer because it stays light outside longer and I can hear the children who live in our street playing out.

I am peeping out of the bedroom window watching them when suddenly his white van comes down our road and stops outside. Maybe he forgot his flask and sandwich, I think.

He gets out of the van and slams the door hard.

The next thing I hear is Mummy shouting at him. I cannot hear what he is saying but I can tell she is terribly angry with him.

I am wide awake now, so, I creep out of my room and crouch by the stairs to listen to them.

He is sitting in his armchair with his head in his hands and he is crying. I am shocked. I have never seen a grown-up cry before. Mummy is standing over him with her hands on her hips telling him to sort himself out and that we must leave now. Tonight!

She gets her shopping bag and starts throwing her ornaments in to it.

I quickly get back into bed and pull the covers over my face just in case she means it and we must go.

I must have fallen asleep because the next thing I know is she is shaking me and telling me to get up. It is very dark outside. She tells me to get dressed quickly.

When I have, I go downstairs and can see straightaway that none of our things are there anymore.

She thrusts my coat at me and tells me to get in the van.

Daddy is in the van already with the engine running. He does not look at me.

She comes out of the house and posts the front door key through the letterbox and gets in the van and we drive off.

I do not know what happened in Liverpool.

We end up living back in Reading in a different part of the town from before which means I still have to go to a new school. Our new house is a bit like the one we left behind in Liverpool. There are lots of other houses crowded into our new street.

My new school is big and there are hundreds of children in my class.

In all the excitement of leaving Liverpool and coming back to Reading, I forget to avoid stepping on the pavement cracks and doing things three times.

"Shhh."

I am woken up by my father kissing my face and mumbling. I can hear what sounds like a little animal crying in pain, there is none, only me and him. The smell of his hair cream and cigarettes chokes me and I start coughing.

"Hey shh," he whispers into my face and the vile night. "Mummy might hear and you know what will happen if she does."

I try to get away from him and his seeking hands that are pulling at my pyjama trousers, but there is nowhere for me to go.

I am so upset that it has happened again and I know it is my own fault because I stepped on all those pavement cracks.

Next morning

I need to make my bed nicely before Mummy sees how messy I have made it.

The frame is too heavy for me to move and I am too small to stretch across to smooth out the bottom sheet and tuck it in by the wall. I drag the blanket from the floor and try to arrange it so it looks neat.

Mummy comes into the bedroom and she looks angry with me.

"What's this?" she angrily pulls the blanket from the bed exposing the damp and stained bottom sheet.

"You wet the bed again, didn't you?" she snarls.

I back away from her.

"No, Mummy, I never did."

"Don't you bloody lie to me, you little bitch!"

She grabs my pyjama bottoms and yanks them down. The tell-tale aroma of pee wafts up from my stained knickers.

"Take them off!" she orders, watching me with her hands on her hips.

Slowly I peel them stickily from my body and hand them to her engulfed in guilt and shame.

"Well, you needn't think you're getting clean sheets. You make your mess you lie in it."

With that, she leaves me clutching my head in shame.

Dirty, dirty, dirty little girl.

I quickly get dressed to cover my nakedness and follow her into the kitchen clutching Glonky.

I love Glonky even though he did not do his job and keep me safe last night.

The dirty knickers are nowhere to be seen.

She turns as I enter and smiles at me.

"I made you a tea and some toast. Come on be a good girl and eat it up!"

Joy sings in my chest. I am not in trouble! Mummy likes me today. I cannot believe it!

Happily, I pull out a chair and climb up to reach my breakfast.

The radio is on and I can hear a song that I vaguely remember from somewhere.

I start humming along as I eat my toast.

I will try to stay out of her way today to make sure I do not do something to spoil her good mood.

I pull a chair up to the kitchen sink so I can wash my cup and plate at the sink. The washing up liquid bottle reminds me of the advert on the telly for it. The mummy is washing the little girls' hands and singing softly to her. It makes me feel sad, a big old sorry for myself lump forms in my throat because I know why my mummy would never sing to me or touch me so gently. I am a dirty little girl because I let Daddy play his games with me in the night. It is my own fault; I do not like it and Daddy says I should because it is nice. It is not nice it hurts.

Thoughts of my shame redden my face and I go to my spot behind my bedroom door to escape my thoughts.

I am trying to capture a blue sky and green grass with my crayons. They are dry, scratchy and rip into the paper.

I can hear Mummy chatting with Babs on the phone, so I know not to make any noise.

I like it better when Daddy is not here. Sometimes he goes away for his work and Mummy lets me sleep in her big bed with her.

When Daddy came in, Mummy told me to get ready for bed.

I could hear the low murmur of their voices in the kitchen and hoped she was telling him what a good girl I had been that day.

She had made my favourite dinner of egg and chips and apple crumble with custard for afters.

I had not eaten anything since my breakfast and my tummy was rumbling so much that it hurt.

I heard Daddy laugh and an image of what he made me do last night flashed into my mind.

My knees buckled and my breath was coming too fast. Twinkle, twinkle, twinkle, twinkle, twinkle. Vile images crowded my mind making hot sick rise in my throat. All thoughts of my lovely dinner fled leaving me panting and helpless.

I creep into the bathroom and splash my face with water. I look in the mirror and see my red face and gormless expression reflected at me. I slap my face over and over making it even more red and pull my hair, with my mouth wide open in a silent scream.

Dirty little girl, dirty, dirty, dirty. Mummy is right, I am a dirty little girl.

I grab the slimy flannel and soap and beginning with my toes start to scrub myself all over.

I must do this three times properly without any nasty things crowding my mind and then I will be OK...the consequence of not doing this properly meant that it would happen again.

I heard Daddy's voice outside the door, so I had to start again toes washed, one, two, three, legs washed, one, two, three. All the way up to my face. It makes me tired and worry that I would get into trouble for taking too long but I could not take the risk of not following the ritual to the letter.

Finally, the worst bit of all but the most important; I push the soap into my mouth, gagging at the over perfumed taste and slimy texture. I rub it inside my cheeks, around my gums and all over my tongue.

I just needed to get Glonk and then I would be safe.

Glonk in hand I went into the kitchen to have my dinner, it was not there. Puzzled I went to the living room where they were eating theirs on their laps in front of the evening news.

"Mummy, I am sorry I can't find my dinner."

"Your dinner is there," she said pointing to the coffee table.

On my Peter Rabbit plate set with my Peter Rabbit knife and fork that my Gran had sent me was my soiled red knickers from the night before.

I was confused; how could my knickers be my dinner? Was she having a joke with me?

I looked from one to the other unsure of what to do.

He pushed me towards the coffee table.

"Eat."

I backed away but he quickly grabbed me, pushing me onto the carpet in front of the plate of stinky knickers.

"Eat."

I looked to Mummy but she was seemingly engrossed in the TV.

"EAT!" he yelled in my ear making me jump with fear.

Slowly I picked up my knife and fork and tried to saw through the material.

They both started laughing.

"Oh, turn the telly off, Ruth love, I want to see this!" he cackled.

She turned it off and both gave me their full attention, grinning and smirking at each other.

I frantically tried to saw through the material, but it kept slipping off the plate.

Still, they stared.

"Eat!"

He spat.

Slowly I put down my useless knife and fork and brought the stinking soiled knickers up to my mouth.

Twinkle, twinkle, little star.

Maxine 2018

The thing that follows me around is high up in the corner of my bedroom ceiling watching me.

I am getting wise to it now; the vile smell that follows me around signals that it is there.

I am pinned to my bed in terror unable to move whilst it casts vile images around me.

Red knickers gain life sized proportions and wrap themselves around my head and throat choking me with their vile stench. I am clawing at my face and throat trying to free myself to no avail. There is only one thing for it; to end this relentless cycle of torment. As soon as the idea crosses my mind the images stop. The constant noise like the sound of a washing machine ever present in my mind only makes its present known when it stops. I look to the corner of my ceiling; it is still there, watching me, goading me, controlling me.

The feel of the wind in my face as I push open my balcony doors is so kind and friendly.

"Come!" It entices me.

"Come with me and this will all be over."

I slide onto the ledge so my legs dangle over the side; only my grip on the ledge is stopping me from falling. I want to fall into the wind, the gentle oblivion that it offers me is too enticing to ignore.

The wind is getting up now screaming in my ears, my hands go to cover them and I feel myself start to fall.

I am jerked awake by Anna grabbing me and pulling me down from the ledge.

She drags me into the bedroom slamming the doors shut.

Panting and crying she enfolds me in her arms and we sit rocking and crying on the cold hardwood floor.

I am vaguely aware of the sound of Vincent whining and the clatter of his claws as he paces the room and the vile smell that emanates from the thing grinning at us from the corner of my room.

Part Two

There is only me and an old man wearing a hat in the doctor's waiting room.

I have made it abundantly clear to him that I do not want to chat nor am I in the slightest bit interested in his prostate, but still, he persists.

Twinkle twinkle.

"Maxine? Do you want to come through?" Doctor Shah asks gently.

I jolt back into my surroundings and realise that I have wrapped my arms around myself, pulling my parka tight and I am rocking gently back and forth.

Doctor Shah signs me off work for two weeks with a prescription of Amitriptyline.

I have not been able to talk to her at all because her kindness and gentle voice opened the floodgate of tears that I had been holding back for so long.

She takes me back into reception and makes me an appointment to see her the following week.

Anna is waiting in her car for me outside, she had wanted to come in with me, but I had refused.

We are waiting in traffic for the lights to change when the white transit van pulls out from the right; I scream and grab her arm pulling her to me. The shock makes her stall the car and she is visibly shaken; there is nothing there.

"I'm sorry, I'm so sorry, I thought he was going to hit you!" I gabble.

She looks at me strangely; restarts the car and drives us home in total silence.

I cannot face going anywhere or even speaking to anyone, so she calls Harry and sends him across a copy of my sick note. That done she takes my prescription to get it filled.

As her car pulls away, I let go of the brave face I have been holding on for her, and collapse onto the sofa in floods of tears. I do not know why I am crying but there is a pain so deep in my chest that I cannot stop.

Hearing her car return I quickly go into the downstairs toilet to blow my nose and wipe my face.

I feel a bit better for the crying and I am relieved that I have medication to help.

We go for a long walk on the beach with Vincent after a lunch of crusty rolls and cheese and I feel a strange kind of calm.

The beach is deserted as it normally would be on a weekday afternoon in October.

Anna is throwing Vincent sticks and as I watch him race away into the distance, I notice a tiny figure hunched on the sand. It looks like a small child from where I am standing, but why would a child be on the beach on its own?

I start to walk towards it but though the figure is not moving, I do not seem to be making any progress towards it.

Vincent comes bounding towards me with the stick in his mouth which he will carry home and take care of until the next run on the beach.

Later that evening, Anna asks me about the incident in the car.

"Why were you screaming and grabbing me, Mum? You realise there was nothing there, right?"

I have taken my first dose of medication and I am starting to feel warm and relaxed. All the horror of the past few weeks has melted away, so it is easy for me to be honest.

"I thought that a van was going to go into you," I reply.

She looks at me puzzled.

"There was nothing there. No van. Nothing."

I wish she had not started this; anxiety starts to knot my stomach.

"I don't want to talk about it right now, but I will explain when I understand it myself," I say red with embarrassment.

As I move to pick up my mug of tea a vision flashes in my mind of an erect penis through a pair of grubby grey trousers. I am immediately crippled with such a sense of shame it feels like time has stood still. Shaking my head to remove the image I try to focus on the mug in front of me. The visions are coming at me from everywhere; even when I close my eyes they are there. I sit back with a scream of frustration and start knocking my head with my knuckles to remove it.

Taking a few deep breaths, I manage to shake it, but I am left feeling so ashamed that I cannot look up when Anna calls my name.

"What is it, Mum?"

She sounds worried.

"Oh, I felt a bit dizzy, got up too quickly," I reply.

I know she does not believe me, but I can hardly tell her what I have just seen.

I make the easy decision that I will not tell Anna what is going on; the hard bit will be trying not to react to the demons in my mind in her presence.

Acknowledging to myself that I am being hijacked with vile images and smells a makes me feel a bit better; like I can have some sort of control over it if I am ready for it.

I just hope I am strong enough to get through it.

I wake in the early hours of the morning to find myself downstairs talking into an ornate framed mirror by the front door.

I have no idea what I have been talking about or to whom, but I am left with a strange sense of urgency and a feeling of impending doom.

I am not letting this beat me. I have nothing to worry about, it was just another bad dream, I berate myself.

I make myself a tea with honey and go upstairs to my room. Vincent and Belle are both curled up at the end of my bed; no doubt keeping each other warm because the room is freezing where I have left the balcony doors open.

There is only one thing that can settle me and that is to watch the sea. Wrapping up in my thickest dressing gown I go outside onto the balcony and watch the waves until I feel sleep start to overtake me.

The next morning to Vincent's delight I take him for an extra-long run on the beach. It is bitterly cold and the waves are thrashing the shore sending up so much spray that we are soaked through within seconds.

In the far distance in what looks like the exact spot as yesterday, I spy the tiny figure. I am determined this time to get to whoever it is.

I get my bearings and signpost in my mind where they are. From where I am standing, it looks like they are not far from the fairground that is still open. I start walking as quickly as I can. This is a small child, that much I am sure of.

Sometime later I find myself going through the garden door to my house.

Vincent has exhausted himself and barged in through the kitchen door before me to get to his water dish.

I am shocked to see it is already two in the afternoon. I went out at eleven and I have somehow managed to lose three hours. I check the clock again but the rumbling in my tummy tells me I have missed lunch and lost hours of the day.

I am beginning to wonder which one of me is the right me. Am I the one in the here and now who pinches her little fingertips to prove she is here? Or am I the other one who wonders around like a lost soul in the middle of the night and sees things that aren't there?

I do not know which one I prefer. The sensation of jolting back into my body and remembering all over again the horror of the last few months is distressing but what about the other one that tries to throw herself from the balcony?

I put some bread in the toaster and make a coffee.

The sun is trying to shine through the wall of glass between the kitchen diner and living room. It sends sunlight slanting across the table highlighting my mobile phone that I have not picked up for days. Remembering my toast and coffee I prepare it and bring it to the table, plugging my phone into the charger as I go. The screen soon lights up with messages and voicemails, it seems I have been popular. When I look at the call log, I can see seven missed calls from my mother and I know without even listening that the voicemails will be from her speaking in her poor me voice and pretending concern because she has not heard from me.

I delete the messages without reading them and the voicemails without listening to them.

She will not give up, so I type out a message telling her that I am unwell and not up to speaking. Almost immediately after I have sent it my phone rings; it is her.

Anxiety grips my stomach and my hands are slick with sweat.

I pick up the phone.

"Hello."

"Oh, Maxine, you answered. I didn't expect you to answer."

"Why did you ring then?"

"I didn't want to bother you, but I was worried."

"About?"

"You said you're not well and I haven't heard from you or seen you."

"I have been signed off work with anxiety and depression."

"Oh yes I have that. Have you got anti-depressants? Oh, Maxine, come to me I will look after you. Give you a break."

"Why would I want to do that?" I retort rudely.

"Well give yourself a break from that house and that dog."

"Why would I want to do that?" I say getting angry.

"I only want to help."

"No. No you don't. You want me there, so you have a captive audience for your pity party so no."

"Maxine, please."

I cut her off. I sit staring at my phone daring her to ring again; I cannot deal with her now. No, scratch that, I cannot

76

deal with her at any time. With that, I block her number so she cannot call me again today or ever.

I sit for a moment feeling relieved that I have finally taken back a bit of control from her. I wait for the usual guilt to creep up on me, but it does not.

Unbidden an image of a child's bruised and torn vagina floats through my consciousness. I am horrified and slap my head to rid my mind of the awful image. The smell creeps up on me and the images come in thick and fast.

NO, NO, NO.

The man's penis through the trousers.

A torn and stained string vest pushed against my face.

A pillow made slimy with hair cream.

Dried semen on my stomach and chest and in my hair.

I scream, punching my own head and pacing around the house.

My heart is going to burst out of my chest any moment.

Make it stop. Make it stop. Make it stop.

Twinkle twinkle little star.

Slowly my heart rate steadies and my breathing slows down. I need a bath; I feel so dirty and ashamed. A sob lodges in my throat and I collapse onto the sofa holding my head in my hands.

I am going mad.

I pick up my mobile phone and call the doctor.

Dr Shah fits me in at the end of surgery but my shame about what I have been seeing and smelling prevents me explaining exactly why I rang in a panic for an appointment.

I know I am a mess sitting there rocking and pinching my fingers and tapping my head. I can see myself and I am disgusted with the self-pity that I am witnessing.

Poor Doctor Shah having that thing infecting her nice clean surgery.

I jolt back into my body with a start to hear her asking me if I had thought of hurting myself.

I shake my head, no.

She gives me another prescription to help with my anxiety and asks me to think about having counselling.

I ask if the new medicine will help me to sleep and she promises it will, but the full benefits will not be felt immediately and sometimes people feel worse initially when they start taking this kind of medication.

Great.

I have no idea how I got to the surgery, so I am surprised and a little grateful to see my car in the car park.

I have lost my love of driving since the white van started chasing me, but I need to get this prescription into the chemist, and I am so tired I am glad I do not have to walk there.

I go to the supermarket to put my prescription into their pharmacy and do some shopping whilst I am waiting for it.

People are everywhere, coming too close, not moving quickly enough or not moving out of my way at all.

I am so angry that I push my way past a particularly slow woman who is talking on her mobile phone and walking at a snail's pace.

"For fucks sake!" I spit angrily.

"Just get off that fucking phone and fucking move."

She jumps a mile and looks flustered as I barge her out of my way, heart hammering, palms sweating and panting like I have just ran a marathon.

In my hurry to get out of there, I go to the self-service till and practically throw my shopping into my bag for life. I pick it up to leave and it splits allowing all the contents to spill on to the floor.

Someone is wailing and it is hurting my ears.

I look over and there I am sitting like a mad thing on the supermarket floor crying and trying to retrieve my shopping from under people's feet.

Re-joining my body, I gather everything up, thanking the assistant for the new bag and red with embarrassment hurry out.

Thankfully, my prescription is ready, so I get back to my car and drive home.

I can see the white transit van right up behind me and the fury kicks in again.

Shouting at the top of my voice I let it have it. I am not scared. This is war.

"Fucking, fuck right, fucking off!" I scream at the top of my voice, as I glare at in in my rear-view mirror. I glance at the road ahead and then look back at the mirror and it has gone.

Home should be a haven of warmth and safety, but it is not anymore. This infuriates me even more. My life has been completely high jacked by the thing that seems to have attached itself to me. I am so angry that I decide there and then that I will not be its victim anymore.

I call Anna and suggest she stays at her boyfriend's house tonight because I do not want her witnessing anymore madness.

I make myself a supper of crackers, cheese and apples and settle on the window seat with it.

The night outside is cold and the wind blustery, a night to be happy to be behind closed doors.

Vincent is still tired from his three hours walk this morning and is curled up with Belle on the rug before the fire. I do not bother putting the television on and by 9 p.m. I am so tired I decide to call it a night.

Double checking all the doors and windows are locked I call Vincent and Belle and we make our way upstairs. Belle runs up in front of us to bag the best spot on the bed. As I reach the top stair, she lets out a yowl of fright and dashes past us back down the stairs. Vincent unconcerned plods back after her. There is nothing for it, I must go and find her if I want a decent night's sleep.

I find her sitting by her cat flap that I have locked for the night. I do not blame her wanting to get out; there is more to be frightened of inside this house than there is outside.

I pick her up and carry her back up the stairs. Near the top she starts to struggle to get away; I let her go. I am too tired to chase after her tonight.

I run a deep hot bath and put some relaxing music on through my speakers. With the bathroom window wide open and scented candles perfuming the air, I lay back and relax. Emptying my mind, I visualise a pure white light entering my body. As I take slow calming breaths, I feel the stress of the day float away.

This is the most relaxed I have felt in an awfully long while. I do not know if it is the medication kicking in or if I am just too tired to fight anymore.

When the water starts to cool, I get out wrapping myself in my thick white towelling dressing gown and go and sit on the balcony.

The night air is cold and apart from the sound of the waves crashing to the shore it is very peaceful.

I climb into bed with my book, but two pages in and my eyes are drooping. I switch off the bedside lamp and drift off.

Maxine 1978

Mummy has left me alone with Daddy. She said she needs some peace away from me and he is busy painting the living room so he can look after me.

I know what will happen, so I beg and cry for her to take me with her. She just looks at me in disgust and without saying anything gets her coat and slams the front door behind her.

I go and hide behind my bedroom door so he cannot find me. I close my eyes very, very tightly whispering to myself, "Twinkle twinkle little star."

The sea is waiting for me, it is rushing up to me making the sand wet. I can hear the fairground; the throb of the machinery that makes the rides work. The smell in the air is of chips and hot donuts. I do not feel hungry, I am simply happy to have the beach all to myself.

"Open your legs."

My father's voice pierces the air.

I am being dragged across the bedroom floor.

I am naked.

He is forcing my legs apart and holding them open. My back hurts, my legs hurt. I do not like it.

Please someone help me.

Maxine 2018

I wake with a start, my legs are being forced wide open, something or someone is crouched at the bottom of my bed holding my legs akimbo. I try to scream, nothing comes out.

Maxine 1978

What is he doing? I can hear him breathing heavily. Suddenly his fingers spreads open my vagina and he is fumbling in his trousers.

Maxine 2018

The stench in my room is suffocating, I am trapped, I cannot move, I cannot breathe…this is not allowed to happen. Calling upon the reserves of anger that is my constant companion I manage to raise my head and recognise the thing that sits staring at me from the bedroom ceiling, is at the bottom of my bed holding my legs apart, staring at my private parts and masturbating furiously. The scream that has been building in my chest escapes on a wave of pure fury and rage and echoes, bouncing off the walls and floor and ceiling until I am spent.

Maxine 1978

I feel the waves lapping at my toes tickling them. The winds ruffle my hair and I feel as though my whole body has turned into liquid. There is no noise in my head anymore. I only hear it when it stops.

Maxine 2018

I wake to the sun pouring through the windows promising a beautiful day. Every bone in my body aches as though I have been in a boxing match. I let out a groan as my feet hit the hardwood floor sending shock waves of pain throughout my body.

I can hear Vincent clattering about downstairs and whining to go out, so it must be later than 7 o'clock, my usual time to get up.

I hurry downstairs and flick the kettle on as I go by to let him out. I am surprised to see that it has gone 9 o'clock and feel a little prick of guilt because I should have been up much earlier.

I pick my phone up and can see I have a missed call from a private number and a voicemail.

I will listen to it when I have showered and dressed, I cannot be doing with any surprises just yet.

As I drink my coffee in the garden a flashback from last night highjacks my mind. I am immediately transported back and relive the horror in complete detail. Feelings of shame and guilt overwhelm me causing my coffee to rise back up from my stomach.

I punch my head with my fist to remove the vision and pace around the garden.

I cannot go on like this it is driving me insane. I feel so angry and frustrated that I am being made to be a victim of something so disgusting I cannot even talk to anyone else about it.

I eventually calm down and force myself to sit and smoke a cigarette. I am going to have to do something because this thing has hijacked every part of my life.

I cannot go to work. I cannot eat meat; I cannot rest, and it is driving a wedge between Anna and I because I cannot tell her what is happening to me. We are usually so close more like best friends than Mother and Daughter and I miss her.

I feel a lot better after my shower and remember that I have a voicemail.

I press play and put the phone on speaker.

"Hello this is PC Barlow from Thames Valley Police. This is a message for Maxine Adams, can you call me back on this number and ask for extension 262."

My initial reaction was one of fear that something had happened to Anna but then the words Thames Valley sunk in and I realised that was the police force in Reading, not here.

Puzzled I ring the number he has left and get through to him straightaway.

"Hello, Maxine, thanks for getting back to me. You recently made a complaint through The Silent Campaign and I just wanted to follow up with you, are you okay to speak?"

"Yes, I am, but I don't think there is any point in this as it was a complaint against my father, and he has been dead for years."

"I understand that, but we have been requested to follow this up by another police force, and as the offences were committed on our patch, we do need to speak to you about it."

"I don't live in Reading anymore though," I stammer completely blown away by the fact that the police are investigating a crime that took place so long ago.

"Myself and my colleague PC Brown can come and visit you for a chat next Tuesday. Is that convenient for you?"

I agree and put the phone down completely astounded that someone somewhere wanted to get justice for the little girl who suffered so much.

It brings a lump to my throat and I sit with the tears pouring down my face whilst I try to get my head around the conversation I have just had.

I take Vincent out for a long run on the beach hoping that I will not see that forlorn little figure by the fairground. The sadness I feel when I see it stays with me all day. Sure enough, there it is.

Each sighting shows me a little more. It is a small child; I start walking and half running towards it but like each time before it is like I am running on the spot not getting anywhere nearer.

Pinching my little fingertips, I keep myself grounded and turn my back and walk home.

Maxine 1978

Daddy has taken all my clothes off and I do not like it. He has made me lay on the dirty bathroom floor and has taken his thing out of his trousers. It is a big ugly thing and I do not like it. He is shaking it and shaking it and telling me to lay still.

"Keep still," he is muttering and groaning and then he goes all still and opens his mouth.

Twinkle twinkle little star.

The waves on the beach are in a bit of a hurry today and the sand is blowing in my eyes…I cannot hear the fairground and I can only smell a nasty smell. I need to concentrate.

My heart is jumping in my chest and I cannot breathe properly. My tummy hurts as though it has been tied in a knot.

Twinkle, twinkle, twinkle my mind is in a vortex and I cannot capture the words.

Suddenly I hear a scream and look up, I am surrounded by seagulls as the wind drops and the waves quieten, and the sand is gentle on my feet. Little star, how I wonder what you are.

Maxine 2018

As soon as I enter the kitchen, I smell it, the vile mix of fag's fart and hair cream that has haunted me lately.

I know the thing is somewhere watching me, I can feel it.

I check the downstairs ceilings, nothing. With a feel of foreboding, I start to climb the stairs.

The stench is getting stronger and so is my terror, but I push on up the stairs.

The thing is grinning and leering and frenziedly masturbating at the top of the stairs. My mind is immediately hijacked with images of a poor torn little female body. The thing is masturbating over her. As I watch through my fingers, I witness it getting more and more frenzied. Until it brings itself to a shuddering climax all over her tear-stained little face.

"ENOUGH!" I scream at it.

"I AM NOT AFRAID OF YOU!" I yell into the silence of the house.

I am very afraid.

I am scared that I have invited this thing in with my challenge as it ramps up its assault of grotesque imagery every waking hour.

It has overtaken every aspect of my life. I cannot go to work. I cannot drive my car. Even going for a walk is dangerous as the white van is always approaching, ready to smash into me.

I have made Anna stay at her boyfriend's house for the last week, to protect her from the madness that is consuming me.

We are barely speaking because she knows I am hiding something from her. I cannot tell her what it is because I am terrified that if I do, not only will I be allowing it to infect her mind, but she will also never feel safe at home again.

I cannot walk Vincent on the beach anymore because I cannot bear to see the little child that I cannot reach no matter how hard I try.

I do not go to bed.

If I stay in one place, it helps. I can see every aspect of the living room and kitchen from my place on the window seat. It cannot hijack me with its presence because I am watching it.

The stained, tatty tracksuit bottoms and fleece I have had on for days hangs from my thin frame. I can smell my own unwashed body every time I move.

I am surviving on a diet of coffee, cigarettes and apples.

I do not leave the house; I am its prisoner.

On the following Tuesday morning, I wake up from my position on the window seat with a nagging thought that I need to do something.

I sit for a moment wracking my brains for the answer.

Pinching my little fingers repeatedly, clears my mind, and I recall with a start that it is Tuesday already, and the police are going to be here at 11 o'clock.

I rush upstairs to the bathroom and get into the shower. The hot needles of water arouse my senses, waking me up properly for the first time in days.

Dressed in a clean pair of jeans and my favourite big yellow sweater, I go back downstairs to open all the windows to clear the stale atmosphere of the last few days.

I have just enough time to dry my hair and put a bit of make up on before there is a knock on the front door.

Checking my reflection in the mirror and straightening my top I go to answer the door.

Vincent is being his usual nosey self and greets the two police officers that are standing there.

They both look to be in their thirties. I am struck that these people who were not even born when the crime took place care enough to investigate it and want to help.

The male police officer explains that when I made my report to the Silence Campaign, that evidence went into a big melting pot that was accessed by different police forces and agencies.

They wanted to know where I was living at the time of the crime, the dates and whether it had been reported to the police.

I explained that we had been living in Reading when I was five and that was when the abuse first started; or when I first became aware of it.

I remembered a kind teacher who used to ask me to talk to her about what was going on at home, but we moved to Liverpool soon after that.

The police were particularly interested in Liverpool, as there had been a complaint made against my father there, and they needed to know the timescale that we were living there.

They asked me about my mother and whether she was aware of what my father was doing to me. In that moment, I understood that not only was she aware, but she had also abused me in her own way.

They asked me if I wanted to make a complaint against her and I immediately said no.

I did not want to think about the things she had allowed to happen to me; it had happened, you could not change it. There was no point in picking at old wounds.

They told me that I could contact them any time of the day or night if I changed my mind.

They gave me a twenty-four-hour telephone number that I could call.

I got the feeling that they would have been happy had I made a complaint against her.

On the way out, the woman police officer asked me if I would like to receive counselling through Victims Assist, a dedicated service formed to ensure that victims of crime receive the support they need to cope with and recover from the impact of the crime committed against them. I said I would as I had promised Doctor Shah that I would seek counselling and had not done anything about it.

She said she would pass my details on to them and I would hear from them in the next few weeks.

After I closed the door on them, I realised that the smell and atmosphere of foreboding and evil had not been present the whole time the police officers were there.

As suddenly as I acknowledged it the smell and feeling came flooding back.

The thing came in and tormented me with its disgusting images and I sank onto the bottom stair in the hallway and screamed out my torment.

An hour later I was sitting in Doctor Shah's surgery trying to find the words to describe what was happening to me.

I needed help urgently because I did not trust myself not to do something to end it.

Most nights I would wake up and find myself either climbing onto the balcony or sitting in the corner of the kitchen holding the bread knife to my own throat; fighting the voice that urged me so kindly to end it there and then.

"I get this smell, this horrible smell that no one else can smell and when it comes, I have horrible pictures in my mind."

"What are the pictures of?" she asks kindly.

I shake my head, no. I cannot bear to put into words the awful images that torment me.

I am crying and rocking back and forth and clutching my arms around me.

"When does it happen, Maxine?"

She carries on, handing me some tissues.

"All the time!" I let out on a wail. "And this thing…this thing is making me try to kill myself."

I burst out part relieved part terrified, I am going to be sectioned.

She sits and observes me sadly.

"Have you tried to hurt yourself?"

"No!" I cry. "It's trying to kill me!"

As the words leave my mouth the vile smell floods the antiseptic surgery and out of the corner of my eye, I see that thing sneering and leering at me from the ceiling.

I jump up horrified; I need to go.

Doctor Shah stands too.

"Maxine, what is it?"

I am nearly to the door; I allowed that thing in here.

"Maxine, wait!"

Doctor Shah blocks the doorway.

I scream out in panic as she captures me in her arms.

She holds me tightly, patting my back and whispering softly to me.

When I calm down, still holding me, she asks me what I saw.

My breathing starts to speed up again and my body starts shuddering.

"What do you see?" she repeats looking into the top corner of the room.

"Don't look at it!" I burst out.

"Please, don't it will infect you too."

"Tell me what you are seeing, Maxine."

She soothes me by stroking the back of my head.

I drop my head in shame and defeat.

"My father," I whisper.

I feel her take a sharp intake of breath.

"Is your father still alive?" she asks.

I shake my head, no.

"He died years ago, doctor."

Going to the sink she pours us both a glass of water and sets one down in front of me.

"You need to tell me what has been happening, Maxine, that is the only way it is going to stop."

I look into her kind and tired eyes and grasp hold of the lifeline she is throwing me.

Nearly an hour later and with yet another prescription and a sick note signing me off work for another four weeks I leave the surgery feeling like I have shed a heavy load.

The waiting room is eerily quiet and only one receptionist remains. Seeing me to the door Doctor Shah takes my hand and pats it.

"Promise me you will have the counselling the police have offered, Maxine?"

I nod my head yes.

"I have made you an appointment to see me at the same time next week but call and make an emergency appointment if you need to in the meanwhile, OK?"

When I finally pull up outside the house, I can see through the living room window that the lamps have been switched on; Anna is home.

As I open the front door she is there. I can tell from the look on her face that she is angry.

"I know you don't want me here, but it's my home too. I have been ringing and ringing today, worried sick that something had happened to you!"

"It isn't that I don't want you here." I begin, unsure of what to say next.

"Where have you been and why didn't you take your mobile with you? Oh my God! You look awful! What happened?" she exclaims when she catches sight of my tear-stained face and swollen eyes.

I put my hand up.

"One thing at a time, I'm OK, let me have a bath and I will tell you everything."

I come back downstairs half an hour later grateful to see that Anna has ordered a pizza with all the sides. I have not felt this hungry in ages and devour my share in silence.

Once everything is cleared away and we have a cup of tea each I try to explain what has been going on without giving too much away.

I begin.

"I have been to see Doctor Shah and she has signed me off work for another four weeks."

"I have not been sleeping very well and it's affecting me, badly."

"Understatement of the year, Mum!" she interjects.

"I heard you screaming every single night. I have been worried sick that you will jump off the balcony or something stupid like that. You cannot keep shutting me out."

"I know and I'm sorry, but it's all going to be alright now, I have seen Doctor Shah today and told her everything. I have more tablets to take too."

I end on a fake little laugh.

"I hated it when you said stay at Joes, I thought you were going to do something, and you were being so weird; I didn't know what to do for the best."

"I promise, I am not looking to kill myself, I never have."

"I wanted you to stay at Joes; I don't want you worrying and putting your life on hold for me, that isn't how it is meant to be."

"But, why, suddenly, you are having nightmares and acting strange? Doing weird things with your hands and sniffing the air like a dog."

"I can't explain it, I don't fully understand myself, but I am going to have counselling and with the medication I reckon I will be as right as rain before you know it."

"I love you, Mum, talk to me when you are ready and let me know if I can do anything to make it better."

"I love you back, Anna, thank you I will!" I respond with tears in my eyes.

Maxine 1978

Mummy said if I am not a good girl then Father Christmas will not get me any presents. She said on Christmas morning all I will find in my stocking is a potato and some coal. I am going to try my hardest to be the best girl any mummy could ask for.

I have a special surprise for her on Christmas morning; I made her a lovely calendar in sewing class that she can put on the wall and write her appointments on it. Miss said my cross stitches were the best she has ever seen and it is a beautiful present.

Every time I think of it wrapped up and hidden in the Christmas tree, I feel fizzy in my tummy.

I am being extra careful to make sure Daddy does not do any of his games that I do not like because that will spoil Christmas too. I am not treading on any cracks at all, even when I am running, and I am making sure all my clothes are very tidy in my drawer. I am doing everything Mummy tells me to do and I try to surprise her by doing extra things like emptying the bin and washing and drying up the dishes extra carefully.

I keep having the same dream that I am on my beach and something is falling out of the sky, I start running away but it is getting bigger and bigger and chasing me.

I quickly close my eyes tight and replace the picture of it with one of the seas. I do not like thinking about bad things.

Maxine 2018

I wake with a start. It is dark outside, so it is still the dead of night. I check myself; can I move? Am I awake? Was I screaming? I do not think so, my mouth is not dry, my throat does not feel sore. I pinch my little fingers; yes, I am awake. There is no bad smell, I cannot see him leering and grinning in the corner of the ceiling.

I lay there for a few minutes savouring the peace and before long feel my eyes start to close again.

I am on the beach and it is deserted. The sea is dark grey and thrashing angrily. There is a feeling of impending doom in the atmosphere. I start walking home quickly in a bid to get away. The sand is wet and sucking at my bare feet. I look down, I am naked, and my body is flat and hairless like a child's. My hair is being whipped by a sudden strong gust of wind, momentarily blinding me. I look up and see the moon, it looks like it is falling. I start to run; but it is chasing me, falling from the sky, getting bigger and bigger as it gets nearer. I cannot get away.

Maxine 1978

It is Christmas Eve! I am so excited for tomorrow so I can give Mummy her present. Even she is happy and smiley today.

Nothing bad can happen, I know this because Father Christmas loves children, and he will not let anything bad happen to them.

Maxine 2018

I wake in the morning with the residual of my dream still fragmented in my mind. I can still feel the sense of foreboding and impending doom.

I lay for a moment trying to shake it off and focus instead on the day ahead.

I have arranged to meet my friend Karen in town for a bit of shopping and coffee. The thought of the effort I need to make is daunting. I need to shower and wash my hair for the first time in a week and put-on real clothes rather than the leggings and hoodie I have been living in recently.

I hear the front door slam indicating that Anna has left for work.

I jump in the shower before I can talk myself out of it and cancel the trip.

I smooth some conditioner through my long blonde hair and get out of the shower to brush my teeth as I usually do; whilst I wait for the conditioner to work. The mirror is foggy with steam and condensation, so I swipe it with my hand to clear it. With a start, I see my mother's face staring back at me. I grab the towel and scrub at the mirror to remove every trace of her.

Coming out of the en suite I smell the vile smell of fags, fart and hair cream; and automatically glance at the ceiling. My father is crouched there leering at my scantily clad wet body and masturbating himself. I scream, cover my eyes and cower in the corner of my room.

Maxine 1978

The sound of my bedroom door creaking open wakes me up with a start. It is Father Christmas!

I know I must be asleep for him to leave me any presents, so I screw my eyes tightly shut and try to breathe normally. I can hear heavy breathing and a horrible smell; it smells like Daddy.

I hold my breath and pray with all my might.

"Please, God please, God please, God, no. Not on Christmas."

Maxine 2018

The damp bath towel slipping goads me into action. Fire is building in my belly; New brave determination propels me to my feet; and I scream at the evil image of him from the very depths of my soul.

I jolt back into my body; all rage spent; cold and confused unsure if I am dreaming or awake.

I pinch my little fingers repeatedly until I feel a measure of calmness return.

I am going to have a good day; he will not hijack anymore of my life; I think determinedly.

Flicking V signs at the corner of the ceiling where he resides, I slam out of the bedroom.

An hour later I am ready to meet Karen in town.

I have put on my favourite white jeans and daffodil yellow sweater. My hair is straight and shining and the makeup I have used has completely irradicated any resemblance to my mother at all.

Karen and I have a lovely time in town catching up on gossip and raiding Poundland for essential nonessentials. She does not pry into the reasons why I have been signed off work but does comment on my recent weight loss.

"Have you been dieting then?" she probes.

I admit that she is right and I have lost loads of weight.

"Not really, I have just cut loads of things out and basically live on apples and biscuits with the occasional take away thrown in."

I laugh.

"Well, don't lose anymore," she warns me.

"You know what the French say?"

I nod and we say it together.

"There comes a time in a woman's life when she must choose between her face or her figure."

"Choose your face!" she says this with a grin.

We part company and promise to meet the following week.

I feel so much better for getting out and seeing her that I am singing in the car on the way back home.

Without warning the white transit van appears from nowhere and comes at speed from behind. I scream and do an emergency stop; braced for the impact and the screech of metal on metal.

Nothing happens; I am sitting in my car with my forehead resting on the steering wheel when I hear a tap on the window.

"Everything alright?" asks the police officer who has pulled up behind me without me noticing.

I nod, embarrassed. I cannot tell him I am seeing things; I will lose my licence or be sectioned and I am not ready for that.

"A cat ran out in front of me, I thought I'd hit it!" I stammer; getting out of the car and pretending to look around.

He studies me for a moment and then with a satisfied nod tells me I can go. I am shaking so badly it takes me a couple of attempts to start the car. Moving off carefully I keep him in my rear-view mirror until he turns off to the right, further up the road.

Maxine 1978

He is telling me to shh shh and putting his smelly hand over my nose and mouth. I cannot breathe.

He fumbles lower down in the bed and taking his hand from my mouth, he grabs my hand and puts it down there on something wobbly and nasty. I know it is his thingy, so I pull my hand away as if it has got burnt.

"Touch it," he mumbles through his dirty cigarette smelling breath.

I cannot do anything but sob.

"Touch it or Father Christmas won't be coming; he doesn't come to naughty girls."

Twinkle twinkle little star.

The night sky is black with big twinkling stars glittering like the lights on a Christmas tree. The moon is big and round up in the sky where it belongs this time. The waves are playful, tickling my bare feet and running back again. I want to stay here forever.

Maxine 2018

I am still shaking when I get home and vow not to drive again.

I slam the front door murderously angry that something else has been spoiled for me.

"I am taking my medication, I am trying, what more do I have to fucking do?" I shout at the top of my voice.

I have truly had enough and cannot settle; so, grabbing Vincent's lead and ball take him for a run on the beach. This is the first time I have been on there in days. The sea is calm and the sky a beautiful shade of blue. The sand sparkles and feels soft under my trainers.

In the far distance, I can see the tiny figure. I am beginning to accept that like the transit van and my father's presence that it is also a figment of my imagination. Nevertheless, I cannot stop myself from trying to reach it.

Maxine 1978

My first thought when I wake up is that it is Christmas morning; followed swiftly with remembering what happened the night before.

My bed is a tangled mess of semen-stained sheets and my pillow is greasy with his hair cream.

I feel a wave of grief flood over me and disbelief that my worst fear came true, he has stolen Christmas. I know I will never be able to get innocently excited about it again. It is ruined. Like a box of Christmas baubles smashed to smithereens.

My body is sore all over and when I try to get out of bed and stand my knees give way.

I sink to the floor and resting my forehead on the side of my bed I pray.

"Dear, God."

"Please do not make it have happened."

"Please make me be dreaming."

"Please help me."

"I promise I will be the best girl ever and never do anything naughty."

"I will not think bad thoughts."

"I will not ask for Barbies or books."

"I will try harder."

"Please, God, take it away!"

I sob painfully and quietly into my hands.

Maxine 2018

A wave of sudden grief brings me to my knees in the damp sand. The force is so strong and unexpected that I feel physical pain convulse my body. Vincent is sensing something is wrong; he runs back to me spraying sand and sea water over both of us. I am kneeling in the sand with my head on my knees berating a God I have not believed in for a very long time.

Maxine 1978

I wipe my face with a swipe of my arm, trying to remove all the evidence of my tears. Mummy will tell me off for crying on Christmas morning; she will say I am spoiling it with my selfish ways. It is hard to stop crying and I cannot leave my room until I do.

I sit for a minute and emptying my mind I recite:

"Twinkle twinkle little star."

"How I wonder what you are."

"Up above the sky so high."

"Like a diamond in the sky."

"Twinkle twinkle little star."

"How I wonder what you are."

Maxine 2018

Feeling drained; I get up, put Vincent's lead on and take a slow walk back to my house.

Doctor Shah had said that I could feel worse before I felt better so it was probably just that.

As I go through the kitchen door, I hear my phone ringing on the table. Snatching it up without looking at the screen I answer it.

"Hello, can I speak with Maxine please?" an unfamiliar female voice says.

I have to clear my throat a couple of times before I can speak clearly.

"Yes, this is Maxine."

"Hello, Maxine, my name is Grace, I have been passed your details from Thames Valley Police Victims Assist. Do you have a moment to talk?"

I sink onto the kitchen chair on a wave of relief.

"Yes, that's fine; hello."

"OK, Maxine, can I call you Maxine?"

I say, "Yes."

"Can you give me an idea of what has happened?"

I have no idea where to begin so I start at the end.

"I am hearing things and seeing things and I feel like I'm being haunted. I wake up every night and I can't move and he's there staring and doing stuff and he stinks!" I gabble away spewing everything, words tripping up on each other in their desire to be heard.

Grace indicates that she is listening with huh huh's and go on's.

"I am scared I am going mad!"

I eventually run out of breath and it feels like I have taken a lance to a boil.

There is a moment's silence and then she begins.

"OK, I get that, and I can help you with it. Listen to me. You are not mad and you are not going mad. I would like to invite you to an appointment with me next Tuesday. Are you available then?"

"I am signed off work so yes I can," I reply.

"Good. Are you taking any medication?"

"Yes, Amitriptyline, Mirtazapine, Sondate XL and Quetiapine."

I reel off.

"Excellent, keep taking them, they will ease your symptoms, but I can provide you with a toolbox to deal with everything that has been going on. How does that sound?"

Her tone is no nonsense and intelligent. I feel as though I have been handed a lifeline.

I agree readily to see her.

After giving me her address, telephone number and confirming our appointment at twelve thirty the following Tuesday she ends the call.

I feel so much better already knowing that she understands; and despite my blurting out the madness that has consumed me, she said I am not going mad.

Today has been a see saw of emotions and has left me completely exhausted.

103

I turn the television on low and settle on the sofa wrapped in a throw. Belle is balancing on my hip and Vincent is gently snoring on the rug in front of the fire. I fall into a deep sleep.

Maxine 1978

With my wobbling chin in the air, I open the bedroom door and go in search of my parents.

They are in the living room; Mummy has a big pile of presents on the coffee table in front of her and he is looking at a book he has just unwrapped.

"Happy Christmas," I mumble going to my place on the living room floor.

I cannot see my stocking or any other presents under the tree.

I do not want to be greedy and ask where they are, maybe they have decided to do it differently this year; so instead of handing me presents maybe the pile Mummy has is for me.

"Oh, here it is," she says in a nasty voice.

"Come to see what Father Christmas has brought you have you?"

"Ruth!"

My father looks at her sternly.

"Hmm, well, I don't think Father Christmas brings presents for dirty little girls, does he?"

Ignoring him, she asks me in a fake kind voice,

"Answer me! What does Father Christmas bring for dirty little girls?"

She snaps.

"Nothing, Mummy," I whisper.

"And why would Father Christmas not bring YOU any presents?"

"I don't know. I don't think I know."

I try to keep the tears that will annoy her even more that are threatening to spill down my cheeks at bay by digging my little fingers into my palms.

"Say it!" she orders.

"Say why Father Christmas hasn't brought you any presents?" she demands.

"Because I am a dirty little girl," I say on a sob.

I feel like my head is going to explode if I do not let my tears of grief and sadness flow.

"Oh wait, look! He did leave you something after all," she says bringing my Christmas stocking, which is really just one of his socks, out from the side of her armchair, and throws it at me.

I feel a painful thud as it hits my leg and spills its contents; There in front of me is all the evidence I need to confirm that she is right, and I am a dirty little girl; is a potato and a piece of coal.

It is over, I am not having any Christmas presents; Father Christmas knows how dirty and bad I am, and my father has ruined it anyway; I tried my hardest to be a good girl and it did not work.

I think of the calendar I made at school; that I carefully wrapped up and was so excited to give her, that is my undoing. I run from the room sobbing.

Twinkle twinkle little star.

I can hear Christmas carols coming from the fairground. I get up from my place on the sandy beach and follow the sound. There is the biggest Christmas tree that I have ever seen. Its lights are twinkling brightly and right at the top is a beautiful angel. I go up to it. I can smell the cool pine scent of its branches on my hand as I touch it. The angel at the top looks down at me.

"Hello, Maxine, I am so happy that you came to see me today," she says in a soft voice.

Her kindness makes my chin wobble.

"I have something very special to give you, my darling girl," she says, beckoning me forward as she floats down to the beach like a beautiful white feather.

I am so mesmerised by the golden glow that emanates from her, that I can only look at her in awe.

I feel myself enveloped into a warm weightless embrace. I can smell the freshly baked cookie scent of her pure white wings and hear her softly singing. I close my eyes and surrender myself to her.

She reaches into my mind and takes all the nasty things that Daddy did last night and throws them on to the sand.

"We don't need that!"

She draws out another image of Mummy saying I am a dirty little girl and throws that out.

"We don't need that either," she whispers kindly.

On and on, it goes until there is nothing left but a scattering of pebbles lying at my feet.

Maxine 2018

I wake up with tears pouring down my face and soaking the cushion underneath my head.

Was that just a dream or did it really happen?

Sitting up I am surprised to see only half an hour has passed since I laid down.

I take a cup of tea and my cigarettes out into the cold garden and try to remember if that really happened or was it a dream? I am searching my memory and suddenly with a thud of sickening reality I remember, that was no dream.

I allow my mind to unearth the complete memory and vividly recall every aspect of that terrible Christmas, on a crippling wave of grief and sadness.

Maxine 1978

I stay in my room behind the door playing with my potato and coal. First, I draw with the coal, it is a bit hard though and keeps tearing rips on the paper. I remember learning about potato prints at school so without thinking it through I try to saw my potato in half with my little plastic scissors that came in a set from Grandma.

We do not see Grandma anymore. Mummy and she had a fall out and now I never see her or get presents from her. It is a shame; Grandma always gave me interesting things that I could make or do. And always the best books, like the Famous Five Adventures and Joanna and her pony.

I manage to break the scissors in half because the potato is too tough for them. They are only meant for paper, not potatoes. That makes me sad all over again because I have broken another link with Grandma now.

Mummy calls me for Christmas dinner; it feels strange because they are both wearing paper crowns from the crackers and he puts a yellow one on my head.

Yellow is my favourite colour but it does not feel special today. I can feel it all crinkly and big on top of my head. It slips down every time I look down at my dinner and I just want to screw it up and stamp all over it.

After dinner he says he will help me do the dishes as it is Christmas Day. I do not want him to help me but I am not allowed to say no or anything. He seems a bit sad and he is not looking at me, which is good. What else is good is that he is not wearing his stupid hat for a change. He probably thinks he is because he has got a green Christmas cracker hat on still. We do the dishes in complete silence.

Afterwards I take my cup of tea back into my bedroom and sit behind the door trying to cut shapes out of my potato with the broken scissors. I can hear them arguing in the front room, he is shouting at her; I cannot hear what she is saying.

Someone pushes open my bedroom door squashing me against the wall. It's him. He tells me I must go into the living room because Father Christmas has been there.

I do not care.

Twinkle twinkle little star.

The Christmas tree has gone and with it my angel. I run to the now silent fairground but there is nothing. I am so disappointed that I sit down and start to cry.

Suddenly, a warm cookie smell makes me stop crying and I put my head up. I sense the soft brush of feathers across my cheek and feel myself enveloped into a pure golden light.

Maxine 2018

The residual feelings of grief and shame stay with me for days, impacting every part of my life.

Have I been a good enough mother to Anna? Do I show her enough love or am I selfish and uncaring? I am no good at hugs, but I have always thought I made up for that by always being there for her, listening, supporting and trying to pre-empt her wants and needs.

I am nothing like my mother.

I go on a frenzy of cooking and baking all her favourites, cheese straws, chocolate cake, chocolate brownies, homemade pizza and bread rolls.

I lose a day and the kitchen looks like Beirut, but I am proud of my achievements.

I suddenly realise I have not given a second thought to the thing leering and grinning in the corner; the vile smell has been superseded by the comforting smell of chocolate cake and home-made bread.

Anna senses the change in me the minute she comes through the front door and smells the air.

"Wow, this looks amazing, Mum! And so do you! What have you done differently? You look like you have shed twenty years."

I steal a glance in the mirror and instantly see what she is seeing. The lines of tiredness and stress seem to have melted away and I look happy for a change.

We eat our dinner and because I am still feeling so buoyant, I suggest we take Vincent for a run on the beach. Even though it is dark, the full moon in a cloudless night sky lights up the beach and the sea.

The wind is brisk and the air is cold. But it is lovely to be out.

Anna starts to probe about the reasons why I have not been myself; I do not feel I should tell her everything. I do not want her to have any of that vileness in her mind and I also do not want to give him the satisfaction of being acknowledged by my daughter.

I brush it off as nothing more than the menopause causing an upsurge and deplete of hormones and that seems to satisfy her curiosity; for now.

We are both exhausted when we get back home so we go off to bed early. She has work in the morning and I have my first appointment with Grace.

As I mount the stairs, I can smell him in the air and see him out of the corner of my eye. I deliberately avert my gaze and take shallow breaths. I flick him a V sign with my fingers; giving myself an aura of self-confidence and nonchalance that I do not feel. My heart is thudding in my chest and my stomach churning with anxiety. Maybe if I just ignore him, he will go away, I think. I am so tired I know I cannot fight it tonight.

Maxine 1978

I go into the living room and she is sitting by the tree with a pile of presents.

"Look what I found behind the tree!" she says with fake jollity.

I do not understand why Father Christmas would hide my presents, that is not very friendly.

I do not want to look at them because I feel like they are spoilt now but I must because she looks angry. My father is not joining in for a change, but I do not trust him.

They like to trick me. Before today, I thought I was safe at Christmas; because Father Christmas would be watching them like he watches everyone, and they would not get presents if Father Christmas saw what they did, would they?

I am a dirty nasty little girl, it is true, because why else did Father Christmas trick me?

I feel greedy and sad when I open my presents because I do not deserve them.

I open the colouring book and felt tips; new slippers and some books but I do not want to touch them and spoil them with my nastiness. I put them to one side and start folding the wrapping paper into little, tiny squares. If I concentrate very hard, I can make it disappear.

"What's up with you? Not good enough for madam, are they?" Mummy shouts.

"I will tell Father Christmas to take them back and give them to a nice girl, shall I?"

I am folding, folding. Folding with my head down trying to stop myself from crying and making Mummy even more angry. Suddenly, my head snaps back with a blow across my face from her.

"Get out of my sight, you, ungrateful rotten little bitch!"

Twinkle twinkle little star.

I am digging my toes into the soft sand and watching the sun glittering on the calm sea. Far away in the opposite direction to the Fairground, I sense something before I can see it. I pull my knees to my chest and resting my head on them, turn my face to look without being seen.

Maxine 2018

I wake with a start, to see my father hovering above my bed as though he is laying on top of me.

111

This porkpie hat is tipped to the back of his head and he is smirking as he flicks dreadful images in front of my face like a pack of cards.

An erect penis through a pair of stained grey trousers.

A child's face being pushed down to an erect penis.

A small child hidden behind a door.

"No, no, no," I cry squeezing my eyes closed but still the images keep coming.

I cannot catch my breath, my chest is tight and will not allow any more air in, I am clawing at my throat and face and screaming the words, Twinkle twinkle twinkle at the top of my voice.

"Mum!" Anna is grabbing my wrists and crying hysterically. "Stop it, stop, you're frightening me!"

I am jolted back into awareness and horrified by the look of fear on her face. She gathers me in her arms and rocks me back and forth, holding my head down into her shoulder.

I feel the panic gradually leave my body, and sniffing, pull my head up to look at her.

"What happened?"

My voice is croaky and my throat feels raw.

She says in a shaky voice, "You were screaming the same word over and over again!"

I feel a coldness cover my body at her words as I remember exactly what I had been screaming.

Grabbing my dressing gown, I steal a glance into the corner of the room and thankfully there is nothing there.

"It was just a really bad nightmare," I say as I leave the room to go downstairs keen to get her out of there.

"You coming down for a tea?" I ask.

She looks at me with confusion written all over her face.

"Is that it? Are you sure it was just a nightmare?" she asks.

I nod my head and try to smile to reassure her.

"I am so sorry that I woke you up."

She looks at me sadly and goes to the bedroom door.

"If you are alright, then I better go back to bed; I have work in the morning."

I go downstairs and make myself a tea sweetened with honey and sit on the back doorstep staring into the night trying to make sense of what just happened.

I do not think that was a nightmare. I could see details about him that I had long forgotten about. The overlarge false teeth slipping about in his drooling mouth. The beady, cold blue eyes sat in pockets of flesh. The awful stink of his hair cream and body odour, stale fags and farts.

Unbidden, long forgotten memories clamour in my mind to be heard. There is the washing machine sound in my head churning over and over, mirrored by my stomach causing it to cramp painfully. It is getting worse; the medication does not touch it at all. He has escalated from hiding himself in the corner of the ceiling to making himself visible right before my eyes.

If I could leave my body and see myself, I would see that I am rocking back and forth and humming under my breath. Twinkle twinkle little star, over and over again.

The next morning, I am up bright and early despite my broken night. I have no recollection of the nightmare nor do I remember coming downstairs and going back up to bed: just an eerie sense of danger and deceit.

I have my first appointment with Grace at twelve thirty, so I force myself into the shower and wash my hair. I want to make a good impression which I know is crazy; she already knows more about me than my daughter and best friend.

I have no choice but to drive to Grace's house. She has a pod in her garden for her counselling sessions. The satnav takes me through beautiful countryside and when I reach my destination, I am outside a gorgeous cottage with a garden in full bloom, despite the time of year.

As she directed me, I go up a small path that runs alongside the garden and ends in a bottle green wooden door with a doorbell. My palms are sweating with nerves as I wait for her to answer my ring.

Grace is a tall, elegant woman, probably about the same age as me with long dark hair and the build and stance of a dancer.

She leads the way to a wooden pod built at the end of her garden. It smells of fresh wood and a lavender and lemon Yankee candle diffuser. The overall impression I have is one of peace and safety.

The hour passes so quickly that I am shocked when she tells me it is already one thirty-five and we have overrun a bit. She did not ask me about the abuse by my father but concentrated on the feelings I had been experiencing. She was not shocked or surprised and that alone made me feel a lot better. She also explained that I had a condition called Complex Post Traumatic Stress Disorder and Schizophrenia.

Initially this diagnosis crippled me with shame and embarrassment until she explained that it was no different to having a disease like cancer or breaking my leg. None of it was my own fault.

I came away with a better understanding of what I had been experiencing. She told me when I smelt the smell and saw him that I was being triggered. She taught me techniques that I could use to regulate and ground myself.

What can I see?
What can I hear?
What can I smell?
What can I touch?

That made me feel better. I have weapons with which I could protect myself from him. I felt like I finally had a sense of control.

She did not react to the things I told her and she did not laugh at me or disbelieve me either. I felt like I had an ally in the fight against him.

Maxine 1978

Today is my tenth birthday and lucky me he did not come and help himself to my body last night.

I have learned that nothing is sacred, Christmas and birthdays do not protect me. Being ill with bronchitis, coughing and wheezing and having a really high temperature did not get me off the hook, nothing does.

I hate him and I hate me. The only thing that makes me happy is stealing his fags and smoking them. I found a field where two lovely ponies gallop about and stare at me while they chew big mouthfuls of grass. I smoke my fags and stare back at them. When I am not there, I am on the beach, on my own. I do not care anymore.

She does not like me.

Maxine 2019

Over a year later and I am still having counselling with Grace. I still trigger but I am getting better at controlling that and my reaction to it.

I feel as if I have opened a Pandoras box and given free rein to the memories that I blocked for so long. The constant assault on my senses have been so debilitating that I have lost two stone in weight.

I am besieged with guilt and shame and cannot face myself in the mirror.

My whole life has been hijacked. I am my memories. I am my guilt. I am my shame.

I cry all the time even at unrelated events.

It might be the poignant music of a television advert; or the sight of horses in the field that I drive by on my way to Grace.

I cry when Anna is at home.

I cry when she goes to work or to her boyfriend's house.

I cry when Vincent flops his head onto my knee and looks at me with his brown soulful eyes.

I cry when Belle grooms him so carefully.

I cry.

I have resigned from my job. There is no room in my mind for anything but the trauma I am experiencing.

I am my trauma.

Because I am keeping so much away from Anna it has caused a rift in our relationship. Where once we shared everything, our thoughts and feelings, there is a necessary distance between us.

I wish I could speak to her about it, but I do not want to contaminate her mind with it.

I also do not want to give him the benefit of her being scared and upset.

During my session with Grace, I had to acknowledge my mother's part in the whole thing. She was as guilty as he was and her abuse was just as damaging as his.

From my first memory at five years old, I had shouldered the burden of their guilt and shame.

A child is entitled to love from their care givers.

I was not loved and only the very basics of care were afforded to me.

I had spent my lifetime trying to win my mother's love and approval.

I do not want that now, so I have cut her off completely.

They are no longer my parents, or mother and father. They are the perpetrators.

I know about the hippocampus and the amygdala in the brain and how the brain changes shape when you have suffered a trauma event.

I know about the stomach brain and the heart brain and how I should take notice of the feelings they trigger; they were there first.

I have done weeks of Cognitive Behavioural Therapy and can understand that I was conditioned to think I was stupid and thick and told lies, to save their skins should a child like me ever have reported them.

I am not stupid.

I am not thick.

I am not ugly.

I do not tell lies.

See? Mended.

We are only just going into the deep tissue stuff.

Maxine 1978

I am twelve today. I do not care what he does to my body anymore, because I am not there. I just know the next morning because of the stink and soreness. I do not even have to try to get to the beach, I am always there.

She still does not like me.

Maxine 2019/20

Grace and I have built up a good relationship. In another life, I would love her as a best friend.

She accepts me for who I am.

I trust her.

We have started a process called Imagery Rescripting and Reprocessing Therapy.

In simple terms, I must face my trauma events and deal with them.

She has set me homework where I had to choose the worst parts of my trauma, write it out and then read it back to myself every day for a week.

Maxine 1978

I am fourteen now and the smallest girl in my year. I have not started my periods and I am flat chested.

See, Dirty nasty little girl, aren't I? I will probably stay like this forever, trapped in the body of a child. It feels like the cruellest trick ever.

It is dark. I am in my bed. I can smell him. His greasy hair smothered in hair cream. His dirty clothes smelling of cigarettes. The stink of fart that always surrounds him.

Mummy, please.

He has forced himself into my single bed. Causing the sheet and blanket to become untucked. I like my sheet and blanket to be tight and smooth. He is too big; he is taking up all the room.

His smelly hair is on my pillow making it greasy and stinky.

His breathing is strange all noisy through his nose. He is tugging at my pyjama trousers and the knickers underneath; I am holding the elasticated waist in my hand bunched up to my chest. My puny strength is no match for him; he succeeds.

He has put my knickers over his face. His fat wormy tongue is flicking out licking them. Sucking them.

I try to get away, but I am stuck on the inside of the bed next to the wall. I am making a whimpering sound like a dog that has been tied up for too long outside.

His tongue is licking my face, my eyes, up my nose. He is forcing his horrid tongue in my mouth. It is too big, I am coughing, choking and crying. He hits my face. He is angry because I am crying.

He pulls my hair back and forces me to open my mouth with his smelly fat finger in my mouth.

He is pushing his thing into my mouth; it is too big and the taste makes me gag. My eyes are watering and I am heaving like I am going to be sick; I cannot breathe because my nose is blocked up with crying snot and my mouth is full of his thing. He is jerking it and pushing my head up and down on it.

Mummy.

His fingers are holding my vagina apart. Poking and prodding, hurting it. He makes groaning noises.

He is holding me by my waist and trying to get his thing in me. It will not go in me. I can feel it prodding, poking, hurting me.

He has his head between my legs. He is holding my legs wide apart, poking, licking and making nasty noises.

He likes to take all my clothes off and makes me lay still on the floor.

He kneels over me shaking his thing. Stuff comes out and it goes on my chest and tummy. He sometimes shakes it on my face. He tells me I must keep my mouth wide open so he can get it in there. He does and it is slimy and smelly and makes me be sick. It sometimes goes in my eyes and makes them sting.

Mummy, help me.

I feel dirty.

I feel ashamed.

I feel guilty.

I sit back and put my pen down, surprised to see that it is the afternoon and the sun is shining.

I wipe my face dry with kitchen roll and sit on the back doorstep with a coffee and cigarette.

The feelings of fear and shame cling to me still so I pull on the grounding techniques that Grace has taught me.

What can I see? I can see the old stock bricks that form my garden wall.

What can I hear? I can hear the waves lapping the shore.

What can I feel? I can feel the stone I am sitting on and the cigarette in my hand.

What can I smell? I can smell the sea and my coffee.

Gradually the feelings leave and I am filled with a sense of calm and peace.

I read the account out loud to myself every day for six days until my next appointment with Grace. It is difficult to read and hear but by day four I am getting a little bored.

I am getting better at going out in the car now. I know the white transit van is just a figment of my imagination and when it appears, I flick it a V sign and ignore it. It cannot hurt me.

I am in the supermarket when my phone rings; it is Anna.

"Mumma!" she wails her voice distorted by sobs. I immediately think something terrible has happened to her and stop pushing my trolley.

"What's happened? Where are you?" I ask urgently.

"I am at home; I don't feel too good, so I came home."

Her words are tripping over each other.

"Okay, you need to slow down and take a breath, breathe, Anna."

"Come home, Mum, I need to see you, I read your stuff, I am sorry I was being nosey."

She is crying hysterically. My heart drops.

"I'm on my way!"

I quickly pay for my shopping and drive home as fast as I can.

She comes out as I pull onto the drive and I can see how upset she is.

"Let me get the bags in and we will talk," I say.

She had come in and seen the pad with my trauma events recorded and read it.

I should not have left it out, but I was not expecting her home and I needed to take it with me to my appointment with Grace.

I explain it all, how unwell I have been, my diagnosis, how my medication was now working and how far I have come with the counselling. I reassured her that I was fine; yes, that stuff happened. Yes, it is horrifying but now all the power was mine. I am facing it all head on and in the avalanche of the sheer horror of it; though it had made me stumble initially, now I stood strong and steady.

It was a relief in the end to open to her, I knew I would have to prove over and again that I was not hiding anything else and I promised I would not.

During the next session with Grace, she asked me to write a letter to the perpetrator and to bring it next time.

Letter to the Perpetrator

I am writing to let you know that I am not afraid of you.

You disgust me.

You preyed on me as an innocent child for your own sexual needs without a thought for the damage and destruction you visited upon me.

You are not fit to be called a man.

You are a weak and small-minded individual.

You stole my childhood.

You will take nothing more from me.

I will not carry your guilt and shame.

I am not allowing you or the depraved acts that you did; to control me or my life ever again.

I am a strong person.

I am not like you.

I am not like her.

I did not deserve this.

I went to the hospital when I was called and as you lay there dying you tried to say sorry. I did not hear you. You could not even focus your eyes let alone communicate properly.

I went there for me; not for you. I wanted to see you powerless and frightened.

You are not forgiven.

I am.

For the next session, Grace asked me to bring a recording device as she needed to put me in a deep relaxation state because she was taking me back to my trauma event.

"What can you see, Maxine?"

"It's dark."

"Where are you?"

"I am in my bed."

"What can you smell?"

"I can smell farts, fags and hair cream."

"How are you feeling?"

"I feel sad and scared."

"How old are you, Maxine?"

"I am five."

"Nooo, I want my mummy!"

"What is happening?"

I cannot answer, panic is building in my chest, my breathing is fast and shallow, my mouth is dry my palms are sweating.

"Stay with it, Maxine," Grace says firmly. "Remember your grounding techniques."

My breathing and heart rate start to regulate in response to her calm and authoritative tone.

"What is happening now, Maxine?"

"He is in my bed."

"Who is he?"

"Daddy?"

"What is he doing?"

"Kissing me on my face. I do not like it. He is smelly and he is making my face all wet."

I can feel my breathing start to speed up again.

"You're doing really well, stay with it!" Grace interjects.

"He's rubbing his whiskers on my face and it hurts; now he's rubbing on my chest and biting my nipples; I don't like it."

I start panting and crying.

"I want my mummy."

"Maxine; I need you to bring your adult self into the room."

A few minutes pass whilst I regulate and disconnect from the child.

"What can you see?"

"He is in her bed on top of her."

"Who is he?"

"The perpetrator."

"What would you like to say to the perpetrator, Maxine?"

I feel overwhelmed with anger and hatred; I can feel it bubbling up in my stomach and chest ready to explode out of my mouth on a wave of pure fury.

"Get away from her now!"

"What is the perpetrator doing now, Maxine?"

"He is crying," I say with contempt.

"What would you like to say to him?"

"I hate you; you are nothing but a disgusting little worm. You do not scare me; stay away from her and stay away from me!"

"What is he doing now?"

"He is in the corner crying."

I spit out with disgust.

Grace gently brings me back into the here and now.

"I want you to listen to that recording every day until next session. Record your Sensory Units of Distress before you listen, during and then again at the end. Bring this with you to our next session."

"You have done incredibly well and should be proud of yourself, this is difficult work, and you need to remember to self-care."

I nod my thanks; the truth is I am still reeling from what we did today and need to be alone to make some sense of it.

"See you same time next week. Well done, Maxine," she says as I get up to leave.

I made a pact with Anna that I would share everything with her but I am not looking forward to sharing this recording with her. I do not even want to listen to it myself, but I know I must if I am ever to get through this.

I stop at the supermarket with Grace's voice in my ear telling me to self-care.

First stop is the paperback section where I find four books in the top ten that I want to read.

I fill the trolley with crisps, biscuits and chocolate that I know Anna loves and then go back around for the goodies that I love.

I stop at the freezers and cannot decide between five different flavours of ice cream; so, I select all of them.

This makes me feel hyper and excited, so I go around again. A new dressing gown for me and pyjamas for Anna. Bubble bath and expensive face masks go in the trolley. I am distracted by the flowers for sale and treat myself to a huge bunch of pink lilies and white roses.

My trolley is full to the brim and I have the biggest smile on my face as I pay and leave.

When I get home, I text Anna to let her know that I am not cooking tonight so she should decide what takeaway we are going to have. She asks me about the session today but I tell her that we will talk about that tomorrow. Today is about self-care and fun for us both.

Still full of energy. I take Vincent out for a run on the beach. It is a cold clear day but the sea is calm. He dashes off chasing imaginary rabbits delighted to be given free rein.

I follow at a slow pace drinking in the atmosphere of peace and calm. I am always struck with how lucky I am to have this on my doorstep.

In the distance, I spot the small figure sat on the sand near to the now closed fairground.

A feeling of determination washes over me, I am powerful; I am fearless; I am warrior woman!

I will get to that part of the beach this time and I will find out who that is.

I plod on determinedly whilst keeping the lone figure in my sight. I appear to be getting closer this time as I can make out that the figure is a child.

After it seems I have been walking on the spot for three miles, I give up and turn back towards home.

This time when I listen to the recordings of my last session with Grace it is easier to deal with. I can see my Sensory Units of Distress ratings are going down much quicker.

I feel like I am finally getting somewhere. The medication and therapy have quietened down the smells and visions but not completely eradicated them; however, I know how to self-regulate when I feel myself being triggered and that makes me feel more in control.

When I arrive for session the following week, Grace notices that I am looking better.

I explain that I feel like I have more control over everything and I am no longer afraid.

For the first time, I am keen to start the next part of therapy and quickly settle listening to Grace's soothing voice.

"Where are you, Maxine?"

"I am in my bedroom behind the door."

"Why are you behind the door?"

"I am hiding."

"Who are you hiding from?"

"Daddy and Mummy."

"Why do you need to hide?"

"I have a wobbly tooth and they want to pull it out, I don't want them to pull it out."

"Are they going to help you, Maxine?"

"No, it hurts, the metal thing he puts in my mouth hurts my teeth."

"Do you know what that metal thing is, Maxine?"

"SHHHH they're here!"

"Who is there?"

"No! Please no, Mummy!"

"What is Mummy doing?"

"Owwwwwwwwww!"

I can feel my jaws being wrenched apart and the head of a pair of pliers is clamped to my tooth.

I am struggling to get away but my mother has pinned me down and has her fingers in my mouth prying my jaws apart. The pain is horrendous. As the metal grates against my lips and tongue, I can taste blood.

"Maxine! Stay with it!" Grace says urgently.

I am rocking back and forth holding my hand clamped across my mouth and crying.

"Maxine, you are doing so well, what can you see?"

I take a few calming breaths, focus on her voice and what she is asking me.

"They've stopped. She has gone. She's left him in here with me!"

I start to cry.

"Mummy, please," I plead trying to open the bedroom door to get away from him.

He has his stupid hat tipped to the back of his head and his hand down the front of his trousers.

"Maxine, I want your adult self to speak to the child."

This instruction takes me aback. I feel strangely intimidated.

"What can you see, Maxine?"

"Him."

"Where is the child?"

I lift my head.

"Over there in the corner, hiding behind the door."

"What would you like to say to the child, Maxine?"

A feeling of overwhelming grief momentarily takes my breath away.

I can see her. She is naked and shivering. She will not look at me.

He has gone, it is just me and her.

I hold my hand out.

"It's okay, you are safe now," I whisper quietly.

She shakes her head and appears to make herself smaller.

"Can I help you?" I ask her gently.

Big wet blue eyes flash a glance at me and the pain and horror I can see on her face is like a physical assault. Her lip is cut and bleeding and I can see a bloody gaping hole in her mouth where her milk teeth have been ripped out with pliers. She is naked and trembling all over.

I move slowly and carefully as if she is a wild animal; the nearer I get to her the more she shrinks into the corner behind the door.

I cannot reach her.

Heartbroken sobs fill the room and the counselling pod. I cannot tell if the noise is coming from me or her.

When I return home that afternoon, I find the leaflet the police officers left with me.

I input the number into my phone and call it.

"Hello, my name is Maxine. I would like to make a complaint against my mother, Ruth Adams."

The recording is difficult to listen back to because her silence speaks a thousand words.

My SUDs rates are at an all-time high this week and I am being triggered daily.

Anna is away on a course with work for the week, I am grateful that she has not had to witness my reverting back. I feel as though I have taken two steps forward and ten steps back.

I cannot shake the feeling of sadness and grief for the little girl.

I tell Grace what has been happening and how disappointed I am in myself, but she tells me it is entirely to be expected. She constantly praises me for the work that I do in and out of session and reminds me of the progress I have made in little over a year.

"Where are you, Maxine?"

"I am in my bed."

"What can you see?"

"Nothing; my eyes are shut."

"What can you smell?"

"I am trying to hold my breath; it smells nasty because of him."

"Is he there, Maxine?"

"Yes."

"Maxine, what does your adult self-see?"

"Get out of that fucking bed!"

I am fuming. My hands are in tight fists and I am consumed with rage.

"What can you see, Maxine?"

"Him! Slobbering all over her. Get Out Now! You pathetic piece of shit. Touch her again and I will fucking kill you!"

"What is happening?"

"HE."

"Who is he?"

"The perpetrator!" I yell.

"What is he doing?"

I stop for a moment, breathing heavily.

"He is forcing his penis into her mouth," I say through gritted teeth.

"What would you like to say to the perpetrator?"

"Get your fucking clothes on and get out of my fucking sight. NOW!"

"Where is the child?"

I look around. He has gone. I hear a mewling coming from the tangled sheets on the bed.

"I'm here now, it's okay, I have made him go away. You are safe."

The child goes quiet and still.

"Let me help you? I won't hurt you; I promise," I plead.

I kneel on the dirty carpet and notice her pyjamas in a heap by the bed. I pick them up and shake them out.

"I have your pyjamas here; would you like me to help you to put them on?"

She slowly climbs down from the bed. Her tiny naked little body is trembling and fearful. She does not trust me; she does not trust anyone.

I hold the bottoms out to her, she grabs them and goes behind the door to put them on.

I quietly go over, still on my knees and offer the top. She takes it quickly and puts it on. It is inside out and back to front but at least she is covered now.

I hold out my arms to her and ask her if she will let me give her a hug. She darts back to her corner shaking her head, no.

I stay with her for ten minutes, not touching her but trying to let her know that with me she is safe; she is loved.

Grace has to clear her throat a couple of times before she can speak.

"That was very powerful, Maxine; how are you feeling?"

I am completely drained and disappointed.

"I don't understand why she doesn't trust me," I say sadly.

Grace looks at me with compassion.

"What is trust, Maxine?"

I think for a moment.

"Love, it is love."

"There is your answer, she cannot trust because she has never been shown love."

When I get home, I throw on my trainers and, ignoring poor Vincent, race out of the door down to the beach. I run towards the fair ground where I spotted the figure sitting in the sand. I keep my eye on it and as I get nearer, I can see more clearly that the figure is a barefoot little girl in a tatty washed-out summer dress.

I am gaining on her this time and the feeling of euphoria drives me onwards.

A tousled blonde head looks up as I approach. It is a little girl of about five years old.

I come to a sudden stop.

She stares at me intently for a moment and then slowly rises from her hunched position on the sand.

I cannot get any closer to her, it is like a glass wall has shot up between us. Crying out in frustration I slap both hands against the glass and sob helplessly.

I stand there for a moment, trying to quell the overwhelming sadness and frustration that consumes me.

I sense a calm coming over me and raise my head.

Her little hands are reaching up and splayed to touch mine through the glass.

I look into her eyes and spot a glimmer of something that looks something like trust sparkling there.

I know what must be done. I raise a hand in goodbye and watch as she returns to her spot in a ray of sunshine in the sand. I do not know if it is a trick of the light or my imagination running away with me, but her little dress now looks like it is glowing bright yellow in the sun.

"Where are you, Maxine?" Grace's voice breaks through the squalor of the bedroom.

"I am sitting on my bed."

"Is there anyone else in the room?"

"No."

"What can you see?"

"I can see the ocean."

"What can you hear?"

"I can hear the waves and the seagulls."

"What can you smell?"

"I can smell candyfloss and seaweed."

"What would your adult self like to say to your child self, Maxine?"

I think for a moment.

"I love you."

"What is your child self-doing now?"

"She is coming towards me."

"Where are you, Maxine?"

I am knelt in front of her with my arms out.

"What else would you like to say to your child self?"

"It is okay, everything is okay now, you're safe."

I drop my chin on to my chest and allow my tears to flow.

"What is happening now?"

I jerk my head up and look at her in horror.

"I have to go; I can't stay any longer!" I cry and rush out of the pod and into my car without a backward glance. If I had, I would have seen Grace is smiling at me with satisfaction.

I do not even stop to change my shoes when I get home.

I am running down the beach towards the fairground and immediately I spot her.

As I get closer still, she turns her head, gets up and starts walking towards me.

I am in touching distance to her now, my heart is racing with adrenaline and I stumble to a stop in front of her.

I kneel in the sand and open my arms; she looks at me with a question in her eyes. Yes, I nod.

As she steps into my arms and lays her head on my shoulder in that moment, we both know that we are finally safe and at peace.

A movement in the distance catches my eye. It looks like someone is walking towards me from the direction of home.

I stand to get a better look; there is a tall slim young man with long dark hair blowing in the sea breeze; my breath catches in my throat as I start walking towards him hope accelerating every step.

Finally, I come to a stop as Magos gracefully steps forward.

Taking my hand in his he raises our clasped fists to the sky in triumph.